"What Kind Of Guy Is He Going To Be, This Future Husband Of Yours?"

"He'll be warm and understanding, have a great sense of humor, be able to laugh at himself...." She stopped, suddenly aware that she was actually describing Kyle. Could he tell?

Apparently not, she realized when Kyle said, "The guy sounds like some kind of paragon. Have you met him yet?"

"I'm not sure. Hey, how come you're the one asking all the questions and I'm giving all the answers?"

"Just clever maneuvering on my part," he stated modestly.

"Do you see yourself being married ten years from now?"

Kyle nodded slowly.

"And what will your future wife be like? Brunette, blond?" Go ahead and fish, why don't you, Victoria? she chastised herself, but she hadn't been able to resist the temptation of asking.

He gave her question some thought before answering. "I'm not sure what she'll *look* like, but I am sure what she'll *be* like. She'll be..." Kyle paused as he realized what he'd been about to say. He'd been about to say, *She'll be like you, Tory.* And that thought scared the hell out of him.

Dear Reader:

Welcome! You hold in your hand a Silhouette Desire—your ticket to a whole new world of reading pleasure.

A Silhouette Desire is a sensuous, contemporary romance about passions, problems and the ultimate power of love. It is about today's woman—intelligent, successful, giving—but it is also the story of a romance between two people who are strong enough to follow their own individual paths, yet strong enough to compromise, as well.

These books are written by, for and about every woman that you are—wife, mother, sister, lover, daughter, career woman. A Silhouette Desire heroine must face the same challenges, achieve the same successes, in her story as you do in your own life.

The Silhouette reader is not afraid to enjoy herself. She knows when to take things seriously and when to indulge in a fantasy world. With six books a month, Silhouette Desire strives to meet her many moods, but each book is always a compelling love story.

Make a commitment to romance—go wild with Silhouette Desire!

Best,

Isabel Swift
Senior Editor & Editorial Coordinator

CATHIE LINZ
A Friend in Need

Silhouette Desire

Published by Silhouette Books New York

America's Publisher of Contemporary Romance

SILHOUETTE BOOKS
300 East 42nd St., New York, N.Y. 10017

Copyright © 1988 by Cathie L. Baumgardner

All rights reserved. Except for use in any review, the reproduction or utilization of this work in whole or in part in any form by any electronic, mechanical or other means, now known or hereafter invented, including xerography, photocopying and recording, or in any information storage or retrieval system, is forbidden without the permission of Silhouette Books, 300 E. 42nd St., New York, N.Y. 10017

ISBN: 0-373-05443-2

First Silhouette Books printing August 1988

All the characters in this book are fictitious. Any resemblance to actual persons, living or dead, is purely coincidental.

®: Trademark used under license and registered in the United States Patent and Trademark Office and in other countries.

Printed in the U.S.A.

Books by Cathie Linz

Silhouette Desire

Change of Heart #408
A Friend in Need #443

CATHIE LINZ

was in her mid-twenties when she left her career in a university law library to become a full-time writer of contemporary romantic fiction. In the six years since then, this Chicago author has had a dozen romances published. An avid world traveler, she often uses humorous mishaps from her own trips as inspiration. Still, she's always glad to get back home to her two cats, her trusty word processor and her hidden cache of Oreo cookies!

One

Victoria Winters was having a rotten day. All afternoon she'd had the uneasy feeling that trouble was just waiting to strike. Who'd have suspected it would strike in the bathtub?

Most days, trouble was something Victoria skillfully averted. That was one of the reasons she enjoyed her work in the protocol department of the United Nations. She had a talent for soothing ruffled feathers. And in a diplomatic arena filled with so many ideological, religious and political differences, plenty of feathers did get ruffled. Often her calm and even-tempered approach to problems was even more essential in the course of her work than her fluency in French.

But today, despite her best efforts, nothing had gone right. She'd left work feeling edgy and discouraged, only to get drenched by a sudden rainstorm. By the time she'd walked into her midtown Manhattan apartment, she'd already decided that the day was past saving. Only one thing would make her feel better—a peaceful soak in a luxurious bubble bath.

It worked. Up to her shoulders in almond-scented bubbles, Victoria finally did begin to relax. Wiggling her toes, she stretched out and settled more comfortably against her inflatable bath pillow. She might have gone overboard on the bubbles, but then she was feeling decadent. That was why she'd set out a can of honey-roasted cashews—her secret weakness—on the small wicker table beside the tub. The juicy paperback thriller she held in her left hand put the finishing touch to what was, in her opinion, the ultimate indulgence.

Within minutes Victoria was completely engrossed in the book—so engrossed that she didn't even hear the sound of someone moving around in the apartment. When she did hear something, she thought she must have imagined it. After all, the strange shuffling noise fit right in with the scary passage she was reading. But her silent reassurances about how she'd double-bolted the apartment's front door fell on deaf ears when she saw the doorknob to the bathroom slowly turn.

It was Victoria's worst nightmare come true. She'd seen Alfred Hitchcock's movie *Psycho* once, and the shower scene had been enough to scare her for a month. Her brown eyes were wide with horror as she stared at the bathroom door, the *one* door she'd forgotten to lock. She was panic-stricken. She couldn't move, couldn't think, couldn't even breathe.

But when the door was suddenly shoved open with what appeared to be the tip of a rifle, Victoria's paralysis abruptly disappeared. Drawing in a deep breath, she let out a bloodcurdling scream. The intruder immediately dropped his weapon, which fell to the floor with a clatter. Victoria let out another scream as a man stumbled into the bathroom.

"Damn it, Tory!" a familiar voice groaned. "What are you trying to do? Make me break the other ankle?"

Victoria blinked in disbelief. The intruder leaning unsteadily against the bathroom sink wasn't some crazed maniac, he was her old college buddy and the apartment's original tenant—Kyle O'Reilly.

"What are *you* trying to do?" she exclaimed. "Give me a heart attack? Honestly, Kyle, you scared me half to death!"

"Then we're even. That scream of yours scared me, too."

As he hobbled over to sit on the closed lid of the commode she immediately noticed two things—one, that he hadn't been kidding about having a broken ankle, and two, that he looked incredibly sexy in a wrinkled pair of cotton shorts. The realization that her bath bubbles were slowly dispersing would hit her later. For the moment she was too busy concentrating on Kyle's appearance to worry about her own.

Aside from a disgruntled expression, the cast on his right ankle and the shorts were all that he wore. He looked exhausted. His blue eyes stood out against the pallor of his face. The golden stubble covering his square jaw attested to the fact that he hadn't shaved lately, and the whiteness of his lips reflected the pain he was experiencing.

She hadn't seen him in a month, and in that time his brown hair had been lightened by the same sun that had darkened his skin to a nice shade of bronze. His job as a troubleshooter for an international construction company meant that he spent a lot of time outdoors, so he often came home with a sunburn. But this was the first time he'd come home with a cast.

She studied the rest of him, looking for signs of further injury but not finding any. Except for the cast, he seemed to be in good shape. In fact, she'd forgotten just *how* good his shape really was! Feelings that she thought she'd come to terms with years ago suddenly resurfaced. She clamped a lid on them. She and Kyle were friends, good friends, nothing more.

A second later she amended that thought. Actually, she and Kyle were also sublessee and sublessor. When Kyle had accepted the position as troubleshooter for Global Construction eighteen months ago, he'd decided to sublet his apartment to Victoria rather than leave it empty for the long periods of time he'd be gone. One of the terms of their subletting agreement was that Kyle was free to stay in the spare room on those few occasions when he was in town. He'd always been very good about giving her plenty of advance notice of his comings and goings—until now! Suddenly aware of her state of undress, Victoria sank lower under the shielding cover of the bubbles.

Her action focused Kyle's attention on her, and for the first time since entering the bathroom he really looked at her. Several things hit him at once, not the least of which was the fact that she wasn't wearing anything besides a cloud of bubbles. She'd pinned her blond hair on top of her head, but some of it had come loose and was trailing down her neck and getting wet. Her face was flushed.

Their eyes met as they simultaneously became aware of the intimacy of their situation.

Kyle cleared his throat. "Uh, I'm sorry about barging in here." He quickly looked away from her. "Listen, I know I said I'd be gone until after Thanksgiving and it's not even the middle of October, but as you can see—" he pointed to his ankle "—there's been a change of plan. I'll tell you about that later, though. For now I'll get out of your way and let you finish your bath."

He tried getting up. But without the aid of his crutches he ended up putting too much weight on his injured ankle. Groaning, he sat down again, looking even paler than before.

"Kyle!" Victoria leaned forward, then realized that she was in no position to give him any help. Her modesty and her bubbly cover were still intact, but just barely. She needed to put some clothes on before doing anything else. "Just stay put!" she told him.

It took her a second or two to work out the logistics of grabbing her bathrobe while pulling the shower curtain closed. Performing various contortions, she managed to get the thick terry-cloth robe onto her wet body. Thankfully, the robe was short, so she didn't have to worry about trailing the hem into the water.

Still dripping wet, she stepped out of the tub and stood in front of Kyle, modestly if damply dressed. "Are you okay?"

Since he had his eyes closed, he missed the concern on her face, but he could hear it in her voice. Tory had such a soothing voice, Kyle thought to himself. Except when she screamed. Then she sounded like an air raid siren.

"Are you okay?" Victoria repeated. "Never mind. Dumb question. You feel rotten, right? Your ankle hurts, right? What can I do to help?"

"How about handing me my crutches? I only came in here for a glass of water."

"I'll get you some water once we get you into bed," she promised as she retrieved his crutches from the floor. Handing one of them to him, she said, "You know, when

I saw the end of this thing pushing against the door I thought it was a rifle or something."

"Is that why you screamed? You were expecting an invasion of storm troopers?"

"I wasn't expecting anyone. I thought I had the place to myself—a logical assumption under the circumstances." She handed him the other crutch. "Why didn't you call me and tell me you were coming in?"

"I tried to reach you a few times last night, but the line was busy and I didn't have the time or the energy to keep trying. I got into JFK this afternoon, took a cab straight here and fell asleep on the studio couch. I didn't realize you were home already, or I wouldn't have barged in on your bath."

"No harm done, except to that book I was reading." She indicated the soggy remains sitting on the edge of the tub. "I dropped it in the tub, and I don't think it'll ever be the same again."

"I'll buy you another one."

"Actually, this was one of yours—that thriller you told me to read. But you forgot to tell me it's so scary that I shouldn't read it when I was alone."

"I obviously also forgot to tell you not to read it in the bathtub," he added with a wry glance at the waterlogged book.

"Listen, I wouldn't complain too much if I were you. You're lucky I didn't throw it at you, the way you burst in here."

"I appreciate your restraint," Kyle said.

"Restraint had nothing to do with it. I was petrified. I couldn't think how anyone could have gotten into the apartment. I double-locked the front door and even used that tricky lock at the top. You know, the one that can only be undone from the inside."

"Very commendable, but you didn't check the spare room."

"I don't usually make a practice of searching the apartment before taking a bath, but I may well in the future."

Shifting the crutches, Kyle prepared to get up. "You'd better stand back," he warned. "I haven't perfected using these stupid things yet."

Despite his words, Victoria stayed close at hand while he maneuvered into an upright position.

"You're hovering," he told her.

"I am not. I never hover."

"Yeah, right," he said mockingly. "Why do you think we called you Florence Nightingale in college? You were always the one patching people up—feeding them your grandmother's recipe for chicken soup and then sending them on their way."

"I never fed anyone a *recipe* in my life," she retorted with a grin.

"Funny. Very funny." He leaned heavily against the crutches. "Come on, let's get this wagon train moving. Ladies first."

Victoria hesitated. "Maybe you should go first. That way, if you slip—"

"I'd probably fall on you and break one of *your* bones. Then both of us would be hobbling around the apartment. No, you go first, and I'd appreciate it if you'd go fast! I'm really not up to standing here discussing it all day."

She saw the beads of sweat lining his upper lip and scurried past him. By the time he reached the spare room, she'd already shifted his suitcase out of the way and cleared his clothes off a chair for him. She'd even pulled a small parsons table over for him to prop his ankle up on. "Here, sit down while I make up the bed for you." The cover of the studio bed was still in place, though it was wrinkled where he'd rested on it. "I can't believe you slept on it this way."

"I've slept on lots worse, believe me." He sank into the chair with a sigh. "Besides, I wasn't in any shape to wrestle with sheets and pillowcases." He watched Victoria as she brought in a pile of fresh linen.

"I'll make up the bed for you," she said, "providing you tell me what happened. How did you actually break your ankle?"

"A camel did it."

She paused in the middle of shaking out a folded top sheet. "You're joking."

"Believe me, camels are not funny. Especially when one is practically standing on top of you."

"Where on earth did you run into a camel?"

"Actually, it ran into me. And I was in Egypt at the time."

"That's right. I remember now. You were overseeing the construction of a new office complex in Cairo, right?"

"Right."

"And that's where this camel ran into you?"

"Wrong. The world's clumsiest camel ran into me outside of the city. Global had another project they were considering bidding on, and they wanted me to check out the site while I was in Egypt. It was in a fairly out-of-the-way location. That's where I ran into trouble."

"Or it ran into you." She gave him a smile of commiseration. "Poor Kyle. Cut down by a camel."

"You would find this amusing, but I can tell you, I've heard enough camel jokes to last me a lifetime. So if anyone else asks, I was simply injured on the job. Got that?"

"Gee." She sighed with feigned regret. "And here I was, all set to sell the story to the National Enquirer."

"Go ahead. Laugh at a man when he's down. Make him feel like an ancient pile of brittle bones."

"You're only thirty-two, Kyle. Not exactly ancient. Not even close. Stop worrying, I'll let you know when you're approaching senility. I mean, really, what else are friends for?"

"Your generosity overwhelms me," he retorted. "Just wait until *you're* thirty-two...." His voice trailed off threateningly.

"Only four more years to go. I can hardly wait."

"I can hardly wait for this damn cast to come off. Global put me on a medical leave until then." Kyle glared down at his leg as if he were holding it personally responsible for his situation.

Personally, Victoria thought he had quite nice legs. They weren't overly hairy, and his knees weren't the least bit knobby. She hadn't had the chance to see much of his legs before, but now that she'd gotten a good look at them, she wanted to see them more often. Disconcerted by her thoughts, she hurriedly grabbed a pillow and stuffed it into a pillowcase.

Little did she know that Kyle was surveying her legs, as well. Why hadn't he ever noticed them before? Or maybe he had noticed but had quickly erased the observation from his mind. After all, Tory was almost like a sister to him. They'd been friends since their college days at Columbia.

Kyle could still remember the culture shock he'd felt at reentering college as a junior after having been out in the real world for a few years. He'd been twenty-four at the time. The other carefree young college students had make Kyle feel old. Then he'd met a serious-looking guy named George, who'd eventually invited Kyle to join a study group. The six-member group had included three men and three women, one of whom had been Victoria.

The six of them had gone on to become good friends, facing exams together, sharing disappointments and triumphs. After graduation they'd all stayed in the New York City area, and they still kept in touch. They'd become an extended family of sorts, giving moral support during the bad times, getting together when they could. With all the traveling he'd been doing lately, Kyle hadn't been able to keep up with the gang as much as he would have liked to. Still, Tory kept him apprised of the latest developments.

"How long until the cast comes off?" she asked.

"If I had my way, it'd be tomorrow. But the doctor at the hospital in Cairo said it would take four to six weeks."

"What else did the doctor say? Did he or she give you any instructions to follow? You know, drink plenty of liquids, take two aspirin and call me in the morning—anything like that?" Victoria's experience with broken limbs was limited. She'd broken her big toe at the age of five, and when she'd been eight her father had broken his ankle riding her oldest brother's motorbike. But those memories were hazy at best. Not exactly first-aid material.

"The doctor gave me some pain pills," Kyle admitted.

"Okay, that's a start. When did you take the last pill, and when are you supposed to take the next one?"

"I took one right before I got off the plane. I was supposed to take the next one an hour ago."

Victoria quickly got him a glass of water and the bottle of pills. She was relieved that he didn't make any macho protests about not needing the prescription. "Have you eaten anything since you got in?"

Kyle swallowed the pill and shook his head.

"Can I get you something?" she asked. "Soup? A sandwich?"

"No, thanks. They fed me on the plane. And since I flew back first-class, the food wasn't bad."

"What else did the doctor say?"

"He wrote down something on my discharge paper, but I didn't bother reading it."

"That figures." She gave him an exasperated look. "Where is this discharge paper?"

"Try my jacket pocket over there."

In his pocket Victoria found two peppermints, a box of matches and a woman's business card decorated with a crimson lipstick kiss.

"A memento from someone at the hospital in Cairo," he explained with a slight grin.

Victoria was tempted to say, *Maybe you should have walked in on her bath instead of mine,* but she restrained herself. She didn't want to sound jealous, because she didn't feel jealous. Or did she?

She slammed a mental door on that question and continued her search through his jacket pocket, almost afraid of what she might find next. Luckily, her next discovery was the doctor's report. "This says you're supposed to take the prescribed medication every six hours as needed for pain, stay off of your leg and get plenty of rest," she said after she'd deciphered the scrawled handwriting. "It also says no traveling for at least a week. And this is dated two days ago, Kyle!"

"You know, I haven't seen you look so disapproving since that time I tried skydiving."

"That's because you haven't done anything this dumb since then. Why didn't you obey the doctor's orders?"

"If I had to be stuck someplace, I wanted to be stuck here. At least here no one will see me make an idiot of myself while I try and get used to these stupid things." He glared at his crutches.

"If I were you, I'd be less concerned about appearing to be an idiot and more concerned about your injury. According to this medical report you've got a cracked *medial malleolus*. That sounds pretty serious to me."

"It's just a fancy way of saying that I broke my ankle."

"Still, you were supposed to stay off your leg and get plenty of rest. I wouldn't call flying in from Cairo particularly restful. What were you thinking of?"

"The cab ride in from JFK was worse than the flight from Cairo," he retorted. "And I told you why I did it. If I have to stumble around, I'd rather do it in the privacy of my own apartment."

"Kyle, this isn't exclusively your own apartment any longer. I live here now, you know. We signed a subletting agreement, remember?"

"Of course I remember. I've got a broken ankle, not amnesia. And I hope you remember not to use the term *subletting* outside of these four walls. If the building manager had a clue that I was subletting to you, we'd both be kicked out of here faster than foreplay in an igloo."

His comment summoned up evocative images that Victoria hastily squelched. "I'm well aware of Mr. Dinkman's views. He reminds me of them each time I have the misfortune of running into him."

Kyle frowned. "He still thinks we're sharing the apartment, doesn't he?"

"Yes, but I'm not sure he's convinced."

"Then maybe my being here for a few weeks will convince him. This might work out all right after all." He cautiously shifted his ankle in an attempt to find a comfortable position. "Look at it this way. If I had to crack my *medial malleolus*, the least we can do is get some mileage out of it. Not that I think Dinkman will give me his sympathy vote. The guy has the heart of a rock. But we can certainly dispel his suspicions. There's no way he can accuse me of subletting when I'm living here." He paused, suddenly aware of Victoria's expression. "You don't look very thrilled with my plan. What's wrong?"

Victoria couldn't say exactly what her misgivings were. She only knew she had them.

"Come on," he prompted, "you can tell me. What's the problem? It's not as if I haven't stayed here in the den before."

That was true, but he'd only stayed a night or two during a period of several months. That was quite different from him living there full-time for a month or more. Victoria was used to having the apartment to herself. She liked it that way. But she liked Kyle, too, and after all, he was in trouble. How could she refuse him in his hour of need?

"It's not as if we don't know each other," Kyle went on. "In fact, it's a good thing we do, or this situation could have gotten sticky."

She didn't need to ask why he didn't think things would get sticky with her. She was "ol' reliable Tory." A good buddy. A regular Florence Nightingale. She wondered why she had this strong urge to hurl a pillow at him.

Her reaction wasn't logical, she knew that. She had no reason to feel insulted because Kyle saw her as a friend. She saw him as a friend, too. So why was she feeling so disgruntled?

"You're awfully quiet, Tory. Feel free to speak up any time here. Don't you want me to stay?"

What could she say? She felt mean for even having to think about it twice. "Of course you can stay. No problem. No problem at all."

"You could try saying that with a little more conviction."

"I'm sorry. Put it down to delayed shock over your unexpected appearance during my bath. There—" She smoothed away an imaginary speck of lint from the smooth top sheet. "Your bed's made. I suggest you get in, you look beat."

"Thanks, Tory. You're a real pal."

"Don't mention it," she said, and she meant it. One more reference to what a good pal she was and she thought she'd scream. Obviously her nerves were shot. There was no other acceptable explanation for her strange behavior. But a few unacceptable explanations kept her awake well into the night.

Two

Victoria was in the middle of the shoulder stand portion of her morning yoga exercises when she heard a loud crash followed by the sound of Kyle swearing. Distracted by the noise, she toppled over. She landed on the carpeted floor with a thud.

"Are you all right?" she and Kyle simultaneously yelled out to each other.

"What was that noise?" they asked, again in unison.

Muttering under her breath, Victoria got up and put a robe on over her satiny pajamas. "What's going on out here?" she demanded after tugging open her bedroom door.

"Nothing." Kyle stood in the bathroom doorway, propped up by his crutches. "I zigged when I should have zagged and bumped into the dirty clothes hamper. What about you? What were you doing?"

"My yoga exercises." She pushed her hair out of her eyes. "Why are you looking at me so strangely?"

"I was just trying to imagine you all curled up like a pretzel."

This conversation was more than Victoria could cope with before her morning shower. "Are you done with the bathroom?"

Kyle nodded. "It's all yours."

She walked past him without any of the self-consciousness she'd felt last night. This morning Kyle was back to being just Kyle. She was relieved by the discovery.

Forty minutes later, dressed for work in a conservative navy skirt and pin-striped blouse, Victoria walked into the kitchen and headed for the refrigerator. Her movements were automatic, her mind on the day ahead, as she reached for the pitcher of grapefruit juice on the top shelf. But the shelf was empty. So was the glass pitcher standing on the kitchen counter.

Dismayed, she looked around and saw Kyle sitting at the dining room table. He'd put on a khaki shirt, but the main thing she noticed was the large glass of juice he was raising to his lips.

"Wait!" she exclaimed. "That's *my* grapefruit juice!"

He lowered his glass and frowned at her.

"Look, you can have frozen orange juice or some tomato juice, but the grapefruit juice is mine." Realizing that she sounded like a nicotine addict eyeing the last cigarette in a pack, she lowered her voice. "I know it sounds strange, but I need my daily dose of juice the way some people need their daily dose of caffeine."

"Sounds serious to me, Tory. How long have you had this affliction?"

She narrowed her brown eyes and gave him her best intimidating stare, the one that worked on even the highest-ranking diplomat.

Kyle immediately held up his hands in a mocking show of surrender. "The juice is all yours. I only had one sip. The stuff's too bitter for my taste, anyway. I'll swap you for a glass of orange juice."

"Deal. Would you like something to go with that? Some eggs or toast? Cereal, maybe?"

"Cereal would be fine. These damn crutches turn a simple thing like making breakfast into a major production. I almost dropped that pitcher when I got it out of the refrigerator. Between keeping my balance, holding on to crutches, and reaching for something, I've got my hands full."

"You're not supposed to be up rummaging in the refrigerator at all. Doctor's orders were plenty of rest and staying off that leg. You're not going to recover any faster by disobeying orders. So right after breakfast it's back to bed for you and no getting up for anything other than the bathroom until I come home for lunch."

"I never realized you had such a bossy streak in you."

"I save it for special occasions." She set a bowl filled with cereal and milk in front of him. "You should feel honored." She handed him a spoon. "I don't get this bossy with just anyone, you know. You want some coffee?"

Since his mouth was full of cornflakes, Kyle nodded.

"It's instant," she warned him.

He grimaced.

"Is it time for you to take another pain pill?"

"You're hovering again," he growled.

"I was just trying to clarify whether your pained expression was caused by the threat of instant coffee or your broken ankle."

"Both."

"You could always have tea if you prefer. I'm brewing a pot of Earl Grey."

"That stuff tastes like dirty dishwater. Even instant coffee is better than that."

"That's what I thought you'd say." She set a mug of coffee in front of him and then sat down to eat her own breakfast.

He eyed her dish of yogurt and wheat germ disgustedly. "How can you eat that junk?"

"I top it off with a fresh banana."

"So that's your secret."

She nodded. "Wanna try some?" She invitingly held out a spoonful of the healthful concoction.

Kyle shuddered. "No, thanks." He took a large swig of his coffee. "So tell me, what's new with the gang?"

"Let's see...George finally got that promotion he was hoping for. It came through last week. Sue's doing fine, I talked to her a few days ago. And Jeff just broke up with his latest girlfriend."

Victoria omitted adding that she'd recently received a letter from Liz, the sixth member of their gang. Two years ago Jeff and Liz had become romantically and sexually involved. The results had been disastrous, and their affair had ended acrimoniously. Unable to face staying in the same city as Jeff, even one as huge as New York, Liz had accepted a job transfer and moved to San Francisco. The breakup had occurred just as Victoria was moving into Kyle's apartment. She could still remember the conversation she'd had with Liz on the subject.

"I'm telling you, Victoria, don't do it. Don't move in with Kyle. You'll regret it, believe me."

"I'm not moving in with him, I'm subletting his apartment," Victoria had explained. "It's not the same thing. With this new job of his, Kyle will be out of the country most of the time. Our situation isn't similar to yours and Jeff's."

"Isn't it? Do you remember the first time we all met at that fateful study session of George's?"

Victoria had nodded. Just five people had shown up in answer to the notice George had posted on the student bulletin board. At first the only thing they'd all had in common was a major in international relations, but they'd soon gone on to form a lasting bond.

"Way back then I thought you had a crush on Kyle," Liz had announced.

Victoria had remained silent, surprised that anyone had noticed what she'd tried so hard to conceal.

"Later on I decided that I must have imagined it, because you and Kyle always got along without any additional sparks. You treated him as if he were just another member of the gang. But I still have a distinct memory of your face the first time you saw Kyle. You sort of glowed."

While it was true that Victoria had been attracted to Kyle when she'd first met him, she'd quickly realized that he didn't view her that way. He might have studied with her, but he'd *dated* willowy brunettes. At the time Victoria had been fifteen pounds overweight, and she'd felt more like a sturdy oak than a slim willow. She'd also had a headful of wavy blond hair instead of the long, dark, silky tresses Kyle preferred on his women. Add to that the fact that he treated her like a sister, and she'd quickly reached the decision that she and Kyle were not meant to be. Instead their relationship had settled comfortably into a friendship that she valued.

She hadn't carried a torch for Kyle. In fact, she'd practically forgotten about the brief crush she'd had on him when they'd first met. But once Liz had brought it up, she'd felt defensive about the memory. "Do you really think I've been pining away for Kyle all this time?" she'd scoffed. "Come on, Liz."

"I'm just saying that if you ever had other feelings for him, be aware of the danger involved. I can't tell you how much I wish that Jeff and I had left well enough alone. At least then we'd still be friends. It wasn't worth the risk. Don't make the same mistake I did."

Victoria had never told anyone else in the gang about that last conversation with Liz. While she'd been talking to Liz, Kyle had been talking to Jeff. It hadn't done any good. The damage was done. Liz had left, and since then Jeff had gone through a series of girlfriends.

The sound of Kyle's voice brought Victoria back to the present, and their conversation picked up where her thoughts had left off.

"What is this, the sixteenth girl Jeff has gone with this year?" he asked.

She shrugged. "I really haven't been keeping track."

"Come on, I'll bet you and Sue have inspected each one of these girls, given her the once-over and then voiced your approval or disapproval."

"Actually, Sue and I have been too busy coping with our own personal lives to give Jeff a thumbs-up or a thumbs-down on his dates," she retorted impatiently.

"Something going on I don't know about?"

She gave him an uncharacteristic brooding look. "Has it ever occurred to you that out of the six of us, not one of us has a successful long-term relationship going?"

"Isn't this a slightly heavy conversation to be having this early in the day?"

"I'm serious. George is too busy with his career, you're traveling all over the world, Jeff is dating every woman in sight, Liz's isolated herself in San Francisco, Sue's still getting over her divorce, and I'm—"

"Yes?" Kyle suddenly looked very interested. "You're what?"

"Late for work." She gulped down the rest of her tea. "I've got to go. Promise me you'll stay in bed and rest until I come home for lunch."

"You don't have to come back for lunch," he protested.

"Let me put it this way—I could use the break from the office. And I won't be able to use my set of dishes if you break them all attempting to make your own lunch. So humor me, okay?"

"Don't I always?"

She answered him with a look instead of a word. "Do you promise to stay off that leg?"

He munched on another spoonful of cornflakes instead of replying.

Exasperated by his delaying tactics, she said, "Am I going to have to tie you to the bed?"

He raised his eyebrows. "Why, Tory, I had no idea you went in for that sort of thing."

"I don't usually," she retorted, "but for you I could make an exception. So what's it to be, Kyle? Do you promise, or should I get out the rope?"

"I promise."

"You promise what?"

"Talk about being suspicious," he muttered. "Okay, okay. I promise to be good and stay off my leg until you get home for lunch."

"Good. I'll put a huge glass of water on the table next to your bed in case you get thirsty while I'm gone or in case you decide to be reasonable and take another pain pill."

"Tory?"

"Yes?"

"Leave."

The apartment was quiet when Victoria let herself in a little after noon. She'd stopped at a deli and bought Kyle his favorite—an Italian submarine sandwich. She'd also picked up a large container of chicken noodle soup. It wasn't as good as her grandmother's recipe, but it came in a close second. She'd even remembered to pick up a few packets of the little oyster crackers Kyle liked to put in his soup.

Her boss hadn't been pleased with her request to take an early lunch hour, but then if he'd had his choice he wouldn't have allowed her to take a lunch break at all. It wasn't that he was a complete sadist who would deny her food or water, but the protocol department was quite small. As a member of the support staff, Victoria was kept hopping—often doing half of her boss's work, as well as her own.

Being able to come home in the middle of the day made a nice break from the hectic pace of the office, especially on such a lovely autumn day. The fact that Kyle's apartment was within easy walking distance of the UN was one of the many reasons Victoria had jumped at the chance to sublet from him. The view from the living room window was another reason. If you pressed your nose to the glass, or better yet, opened the window and leaned outside, you were rewarded with a lovely view of the East River. And last but certainly not least, the rent was affordable—but only because Kyle had lived there for seven years and rent control limited the increases. Newer tenants in the building were paying well over a thousand dollars a month, which was the main reason the building manager, Mr. Dinkman, was so eager to get rid of Kyle. If he caught Kyle breaking the lease, he could evict him and double the income he was getting from the unit.

The apartment itself was large by New York City standards, because the building had been built during the 1920s, before space had become such an expensive luxury. The furnishings were a combination of hers and Kyle's—the little things were hers, the big items were Kyle's. Since Mr. Dinkman would have gotten suspicious if they'd started moving Kyle's overstuffed sofa out and her delicate floral-print couch in, she'd ended up putting most of her furniture in storage.

Still, she'd managed to put her own stamp on the otherwise masculine, basic-beige living room. The lovely end table in solid mahogany was hers, as were the handwoven rug under the coffee table and the apricot throw pillows on the couch. As Kyle often said, anything with any color belonged to Victoria. Which meant that the patterned umbrella stand lying on its side was also hers.

Kyle must have knocked it over, which meant he hadn't spent the morning resting the way he'd promised he would. She found him lying on the bed in the den, innocently reading a magazine. The khaki shorts he wore matched his shirt and made him look as if he'd been on safari.

"Have a good day?" he asked her.

"So far, so good. How about you? How did you spend your morning?"

"Very quietly." He tossed the magazine aside. "I rested."

Victoria's eyebrows rose. "Really? Was that before or after you hit the umbrella stand?"

"Okay, I confess. I went to the front door. So shoot me."

"Don't think I'm not tempted," she muttered in exasperation. "I'm beginning to sympathize with the camel that ran into you. You promised you'd stay in bed."

"And I kept that promise. But someone was pounding on the front door. It's a good thing I answered it, because it turned out to be Dinkman with some lame excuse about checking on the hot water. The truth is, he came to check on me. I told him how much I appreciated his deep concern for his tenants and told him that was one of the many reasons I'd be renewing my lease next year." Kyle grinned. "He left before I could give him any more bad news."

"Do you think he'll leave us alone now?"

Kyle shook his head. "I may have won the latest battle, but the war isn't over yet." He switched his attention to the bag she held. "What have you got there? Lunch?"

"That's right. Chicken noodle soup and an Italian sub from the deli. I even remembered your oyster crackers."

"What a pal."

"Yeah, I am, aren't I?" Today his comment pleased her, while yesterday it had disturbed her. Her nerves must have recovered.

As they ate, Victoria filled him in on some of the things going on in the office. Kyle had always been a good listener, and this afternoon was no exception. The time flew by.

Glancing down at her watch, Victoria exclaimed, "I've got to go or I'll be late. Do you need anything before I leave?"

"Other than a new leg, no."

She left without telling him that she thought his legs were just fine the way they were, cast and all.

Kyle was on the phone when she got home from work later that evening. She could hear his raised voice echoing down the hallway. "Very funny, George. You wouldn't be laughing if you were in this situation." A pause. "Yeah, maybe you're right. Maybe Jeff would be able to give me some advice. Although the way he's been going through women lately he's hardly an expert on the subject." Another pause. "I know, but you've got to admit, he's not always the most tactful of guys. No, I think a woman's opinion is called for here. I'll ask Tory."

"Ask me what?" she inquired from the doorway into his room.

"I'll talk to you later, George. Bye." Kyle hung up and said, "That was George."

"So I gathered. What's this all about?"

"I've got a favor to ask you, Tory."

"Oh, no, you don't." She came into the room and sank into a chair. "The last time you had that look in your eye you almost got us both arrested."

"If you're referring to that time I tried to get my own letter back out of the mail box on the corner..."

"I am."

"...I did not almost get us arrested. That cop was very understanding once I explained the situation to him."

"The only reason he let you off with a warning was because I sweet-talked him out of it," she retorted.

"That's what I mean. You've got such a way with people, you always know the right thing to say."

"Which is why I'm saying no. Whatever scheme you've got up your sleeve this time, you can count me out."

"But you haven't even heard me out yet."

"I don't need to. That gleam in your eye tells me all I need to know."

"This is serious, Tory. My entire professional future could be at stake here."

She sighed. "Okay, what'd you do this time?"

"I didn't do anything. That's the problem. There's a certain lady who'd like me to do a lot of things I don't think her husband would approve of. And her husband happens to be one of Global's senior vice presidents."

"Let me get this straight. You're being chased by your boss's wife?"

"No, I'm being chased by my *boss's* boss's wife. Without going into detail, suffice it to say that I met her at the company headquarters here a few months ago and she hasn't given me a moment's peace since. I've only been back in town one day, and already she's hot on my trail."

"And you're trying to come up with a polite way of telling her to get lost?"

Kyle nodded, grateful that she'd caught on so quickly.

"I don't know. She sounds pretty persistent to me. What did she do today? Call or come for a visit?"

"She called and told me she was on her way over—'to soothe my fevered brow' was the way she put it. I told her I'd picked up a bug in the hospital in Cairo and didn't want her catching it. I finally convinced her not to come over, but it was close."

"You want my advice?"

"Yes."

"Tell her to buzz off. I don't think she's going to take a hint, Kyle. You're going to have to be blunt."

"You know what happened to the last guy who was blunt about refusing Angelica Van Horne's attentions?

He ended up being transferred to a project in the Arctic Circle."

"Sounds like a case of sexual harassment to me. Definitely illegal."

"I don't want to sue her, I just want to get rid of her. Gently. Politely. Without any fuss."

"If I didn't know you better, Kyle, I'd say you were blushing."

He glared at her. "But since you do know me better you're not about to make such a ridiculous assertion, right?"

"Absolutely. I know better." Her expression made it clear that she was on the verge of laughter.

"George was right," Kyle muttered. "I should talk to Jeff about this. Maybe he'll take it seriously, since it's obvious you don't."

"I was only kidding," she said.

"It's too late to apologize."

"I wasn't apologizing."

"Then you should be. Do I make fun of you when you ask me for help?"

"Yes."

"Name one occasion."

"I could name twenty, but then we'd never eat supper. You call Jeff and ask for his expert opinion. I'm going to go put two steaks under the broiler."

When she returned to the den forty minutes later, Kyle was grinning like the Cheshire cat.

"I presume you and Jeff came up with a brilliant plan?"

Kyle nodded.

"Well?" She set two dishes—each one holding a generous helping of steak, boiled potatoes and tossed salad—

on the TV tables she and Kyle had used at lunch. "Are you going to let me in on it?"

"Sure. It's a simple plan, really. I should have thought of it myself."

"So, don't keep me in suspense any longer." She sat down and speared a piece of lettuce with her fork. "What is this master plan of yours?"

"Simple. You and I become lovers!"

Three

Victoria was stunned, so stunned that she coughed and almost swallowed her salad the wrong way. Kyle was sitting close enough that he was able to lean over and pat her on the back.

"Are you okay?" he asked in a concerned voice.

She nodded.

Reassured, Kyle went on to clarify his earlier statement. "I didn't mean that you and I would actually become lovers, just that we'd put on an act to convince Angelica."

"I knew that," she retorted. But she had to admit that his original announcement had left her shaken. For one brief moment she'd thought that he was serious. And that moment had been enough to make her realize that she'd been kidding herself. Her emotions weren't back to normal. The excitement, anticipation and confusion had all returned. The straightforward, comfortable road she'd been traveling as Kyle's pal suddenly had unexpected curves in it.

"What do you think of my plan?" he asked.

Victoria recognized trouble when she saw it. "I don't think I'm the right person to help you with this problem. Why don't you enlist one of your girlfriends to help you out?" She knew he dated several women whenever he was in the city. "I'm sure one of them would be delighted to help you."

"They're also likely to start getting ideas and hearing wedding bells. No, you're the perfect candidate. You won't go all sentimental on me."

His comment irked her. Ol' reliable, dependable Tory would never do something stupid like getting sentimental. What did he think she was, an unemotional machine?

"Well?" he prompted. "What do you say?"

"I don't like the idea."

"I didn't like the idea of going to that diplomatic thing with you, but I did it. In fact, now that I think about it, that situation was very similar to this one. You were having trouble with that overamorous diplomat, and I helped you out, remember?"

Victoria remembered the occasion well. Kyle had ended up dating one of the women he'd met at the party, and she'd ended up going home alone. But then, she'd been going home alone a lot lately—by choice.

"That situation wasn't anything like this," she told him. "You weren't there as my date or my lover."

"So you told the guy I was your brother and that I had a black belt in karate. What difference does it make? It wasn't the truth."

He had her there, she admitted silently.

"All right, I'll think about it," she said.

Kyle knew when he was ahead, and he didn't press the issue.

As he went on to talk about other things, Victoria found herself watching him. She discovered that she was seeing him in a new way, noticing things she never had before—details about the way he looked. He had a rugged face, with a jaw that she'd have called stubbornly square. She'd heard other women refer to his hooded blue eyes as "bedroom eyes." Maybe it was their downward slant, or maybe it was the naughty glint they frequently had. She'd long ago acknowledged that he had sexy eyes and had simply dismissed the fact from her mind. Instead she'd focused on the laugh lines fanning from the corners of his eyes. It had seemed much safer.

Kyle's sense of humor was one of the things she liked best about him. He had the ability to laugh at himself, an ability she'd found lacking in a great many of the upwardly mobile men she dated. In fact, she found a lot of things lacking in her dates once she began comparing them to Kyle. They weren't as much fun to be with, as understanding. They were too tall or too short, too pushy or too wimpy. Now that she thought about it, she realized that Kyle's image had begun to overshadow the other men in her life.

It was time she finally admitted it. Despite her best intentions and efforts, her feelings toward Kyle were *not* one hundred percent platonic. The question was, what was she going to do about it? After seeing what had happened between Liz and Jeff, she knew she didn't want to risk losing the friendship she and Kyle shared. She had to get over this crush or whatever it was before it jeopardized their friendship.

Her options were pretty clear. She could ignore the feelings and hope they went away. However, experience had taught Victoria that shoving problems under a mental rug usually only made them multiply. Or she could play a game of make-believe with Kyle and get these feelings out of her system once and for all.

The more she thought about it, the more convinced she became that posing as Kyle's lover might be the best way to erase her crush. Crushes were mere romantic daydreams—wanting someone who was out of reach. Keeping that in mind, it stood to reason that having Kyle act as if he were interested in her would destroy his unattainable image. He'd be just another guy, not one she once had a crush on. She'd satisfy the curiosity left over from her college days and affirm—reaffirm—that she preferred his friendship to anything else. It all sounded very neat and tidy.

"Okay, I agree," she decided after finishing dinner. "I'll go along with your plan."

"Great."

"What exactly do I have to do?"

"Nothing very difficult," he assured her. "The next time Angelica calls I'll let her come over and have her meet you. Once she sees that I'm already involved with someone, Angelica will go hunting elsewhere. She only goes after unattached men."

"How commendable of her," Victoria murmured cynically. "I suppose one has to draw the line somewhere. It's a pity Angelica didn't draw it on the side of being faithful to her husband."

"I agree, but that's their problem. My problem is keeping her away from me."

"Hopefully, this plan will work." Victoria was hopeful that her own problem would resolve itself, as well.

But as is often the case with master plans, things did not go as smoothly or move as quickly as intended. Angelica didn't call. Not that night, not the next day, not the next night. No sign of her. It was very anticlimactic.

As if waiting for Angelica to call weren't enough, Victoria's patience was also being tested by the daily adjustments she'd had to make since Kyle had moved in with her. Having him in the apartment meant that she couldn't do a lot of the things she normally did, things she didn't necessarily want an audience for. Like creeping into the kitchen to raid a carton of chocolate chocolate-chip ice cream at three in the morning. Or eating breakfast in her underwear. Or wearing a ratty old robe when she got out of the shower. Or walking around with hot curlers in her hair.

Then there was her yoga. Since yoga was not meant to be a spectator sport and she didn't want Kyle walking in on her while she was in a shoulder-stand position, she had to do her morning ritual in the smaller confines of her bedroom instead of the living room. Because there wasn't enough room to really stretch out without hitting the bed or the dresser, she invariably ended up bumping into one piece of furniture or another.

All things considered, however, she had to admit that they were getting on pretty well. A new routine was gradually developing. She'd get up first, shower and get ready for work. While she made breakfast, Kyle would get up and take his shower, no easy feat for a man with his right ankle in a cast.

Victoria had come up with the idea of putting a plastic chair in the bathtub. That way Kyle could sit under the shower while keeping his right ankle outside of the tub and away from the water. She knew from his disgruntled expression that the chair would soon be going, but for the time being the system was working well enough.

She still came home for lunch, more for her own benefit than for Kyle's. His streak of independence, which had been dulled somewhat by pain pills and exhaustion, had returned in full force. He was impatient with his halting progress on the crutches and frequently threatened to toss them out the window.

Victoria remained calm. Her reminder of the dangers such an act would pose to unsuspecting pedestrians below had prevented him from carrying out his threat. But it hadn't improved his patience any.

Kyle's spirits were lifted the next night when the gang came over for an impromptu cast-signing party in his honor. Jeff, George and Sue brought various munchies and drinks. Kyle sat in his favorite chair, an overstuffed recliner that had seen better days, while Sue bent over his ankle, struggling for something inspiring to write on his cast. Jeff and George sat on the couch, sipping their beers and sticking potato chips into a bowl of Sue's famous curry dip that Victoria had just set on the coffee table.

"So you were injured in the line of duty, huh?" Jeff was saying.

"That's right." Kyle didn't go into any details, and a look in Victoria's direction warned her not to elaborate. Changing the subject, he said, "What are you writing on there, Sue? Your life story?"

"Nothing that dramatic, I'm afraid. I wrote 'Battered but not beaten!'" She capped the pen and tossed it across the room to Jeff. "Your turn."

Jeff came over and wrote something in Latin that had Kyle laughing uncontrollably.

"What's it mean?" Sue asked, looking over Jeff's shoulder.

Jeff shook his head. "I can't tell you."

Victoria gave him a sardonic look. "Let me guess. It loses something in the translation, right?"

"Right." Jeff handed the pen over to George.

"So, Kyle, how's the situation going with the man-eater?" George asked as he began drawing a cartoon face on the cast.

"The man-eater?" Sue's curiosity was aroused. "I'm missing something here. Fill me in."

"Kyle's being chased by his boss's wife," George replied.

Victoria immediately corrected him. "No, it's Kyle's *boss's* boss's wife."

"Would you guys quit talking about me as if I weren't here?" Kyle growled.

"Sure thing," Sue said before turning to George. "Go on. Tell me more."

Seeing the warning glint in Kyle's eye, George hastily denied having anything else to say.

"How come I'm the last to know these things?" Sue demanded.

"Because you live clear out in Brooklyn," Jeff replied. "Now, if you'd move back into Manhattan you'd be able to keep up with world events."

His comment sparked a debate about the advantages of living in Brooklyn versus those of staying in Manhattan. It was an old argument, with Sue and Victoria taking up the cause of Brooklyn while George and Jeff hung tough on the side of Manhattan. Referee Kyle declared a tie after several minutes of heated and sometimes hilariously funny discussion.

"You call that a tie?" Jeff protested. "We were winning by a mile!"

"The referee's decision is final," Kyle stated as he helped himself to more chips and dip.

The conversation turned to reminiscences about old college days, and one recollection led to another until the room was filled with cries of "What about the time—!" and "Do you remember when—?"

"Time out," Victoria finally gasped, wiping away tears of mirth from the corners of her eyes. "Would any of you nuts like some coffee?"

Four hands went up.

"I'll help you," Sue offered. "Instant or brewed?" she asked once they were in the kitchen.

Victoria grinned. "Let's be daring and try Kyle's fancy coffee maker."

"I've got one of these things at home. They're not as complicated as they look." Sue showed Victoria how the machine worked. While they were waiting for the coffee to finish dripping, she said, "So tell me, how are you adjusting to having Kyle here all the time?"

"It's been...different. Sharing an apartment with a man is not the same as sharing it with a woman. And I have to say that I did get spoiled having the place to myself most of the time. But so far we're doing all right. We're adjusting."

"What about the building manager?" Sue knew about Mr. Dinkman's eagerness to get rid of them. "Has he given you any more trouble?"

"Not since Kyle came back. That's one good thing that's come out of this."

"What about Madame Man-eater? What's Kyle going to do about her?"

Victoria set five cups on matching saucers before answering. "He's got a plan."

"Uh-oh." Sue rolled her eyes. "Kyle's roped you in on another one of his schemes?"

Victoria smiled at her friend's choice of words. "Now let's be fair. I've probably come up with as many wild schemes as Kyle has—but don't tell him that." She didn't want him reminded of the troubles she'd gotten into over the years. She'd never hear the end of it. "He's helped me out of a bind or two, so I'm just returning the favor."

"By doing what?"

"By pretending that I'm his live-in girlfriend. It seemed like a good way to get rid of the lady in question."

"I'd say the term lady was what was in question here," Sue retorted. "What kind of woman would chase after her husband's employees?"

"I don't know. An aggressive woman, I guess. I think Kyle just wants to get rid of her without a big scene. You know how he hates scenes."

"I seem to recall him causing a few in his time," Sue pointed out.

"Maybe I should have said he doesn't like having to hurt someone's feelings."

"I wouldn't say that, either," Sue said. "I've known him to be pretty brutal when he has to be. But never with anyone he cared about, and never with anyone who didn't deserve it."

"You're right, come to think of it. Usually Kyle is perfectly able to take care of things himself. But in this case he needs me."

"How do you feel about pretending to be involved with Kyle?" Sue asked.

"How should I feel? It's no big deal. As I said, I'm just helping him out of a bind, that's all."

"Are you sure?"

"Positive. Why the third degree?"

"I'd just hate to see you end up like Liz. I got a letter from her last week. She's still pretty bitter about Jeff."

"I heard from her, too," Victoria said. "But you don't have to worry, I've got no intention of ending up like Liz."

In the living room, Jeff was talking about Angelica. "Hey, if you don't want her, send her my way. She isn't *my* boss's boss's wife."

"That doesn't mean her husband wouldn't come after you with a double-barreled shotgun," the ever-practical George retorted. "Besides, you're already seeing so many women you can hardly keep their names straight. Don't push your luck."

"Kyle's the lucky one, having Victoria run interference for him," Jeff said.

"You make it sound like I can't fight my own battles." Kyle was terse.

"Hey, I didn't mean it that way, buddy," Jeff hastily assured him. "It's a great plan, so long as Victoria doesn't read anything romantic into it."

"Tory and I understand each other," Kyle stated.

"Yeah, that's what I thought about Liz and me," Jeff muttered, "and look what happened to us."

There was an awkward silence, as if they all regretted getting into such a sticky topic.

"Hey, what about those Giants?" George exclaimed in the boisterous tone of one eager to change the subject. "Think they'll make it to the play-offs?"

By the time Sue and Victoria brought in the coffee, the conversation was firmly centered on football.

"It was fun seeing the gang again, wasn't it?" Victoria said after Sue, George and Jeff had all gone home.

Kyle nodded. "It's been a long time since we've all gotten together."

"Yes, it has." She gathered up the few drink coasters left on the coffee table.

"Do you realize that you're the only one who didn't sign my cast?" Kyle asked her.

Victoria was strangely reluctant to add her signature to the rest. Besides, she didn't know what to write. "You've got enough graffiti on there already. You don't need me adding any more."

"I'm not sure George would appreciate you referring to his cartoon as graffiti. After all, his caricatures have graced the paper place mats of fast-food joints all over this city."

"I know. Whenever we go out he's always doodling on something—paper napkins, paper towels, newspapers, magazines. You'd never think to look at him that he'd be the creative, artistic type."

"Looks can be deceptive," he murmured.

"What does Angelica look like?"

Her question surprised him. "What makes you ask?"

Victoria shrugged. "Curiosity. I like to know what I'm dealing with."

"Maybe you won't have to deal with her after all. It's been what, two days now? And no calls, no flowers—"

"Flowers? She's sent you flowers?"

Kyle grimaced. "Yeah, she sent some to me when I was in the hospital. But maybe she's gotten the message that I'm not interested and she's moved on to someone else."

"Maybe." But Victoria didn't really think so. A woman who sent flowers all the way to an Egyptian hospital room sounded pretty determined.

The weather forecast had promised that the next day would be clear and sunny, but as usual it was wrong on both counts. It was cool and rainy, with an autumn nip in the air that made Victoria feel homesick for Vermont. The leaves on the trees there would be turning by now. She missed the brilliant display of colors, the vibrant reds, the bright yellows. At the moment the only splash of yellow she saw was the sea of yellow taxis clogging First Avenue. The only flash of red came from the stoplights holding up traffic.

As Victoria waited impatiently for the light to change, she wisely kept her distance from the curb, where passing traffic was splashing water onto those less prudent. She was on her way home for lunch again, a nice hot lunch—her homemade beef stew, left over from supper last night. She could taste it already.

The light changed. Victoria moved forward, only to get drenched as a car ran the red light, plowed through a huge puddle of water and skidded around the corner. Muddy water dripped down her legs and into her shoes. Her raincoat was sticking wetly to her dress, and she felt as though her panty hose were plastered to her skin. Even her hair had gotten wet.

Luckily, she was only a block from home. Her favorite pair of shoes squished with every step she took, and she doubted that they'd ever be the same. Beige leather and dirty water didn't mix very well.

Bernie, the apartment doorman, clucked disapprovingly when he saw her. "Now, miss, I told you to take an umbrella when you left this morning."

She didn't have the energy to tell him she did have an umbrella. Besides, she was afraid that if she opened her mouth she'd either scream or cry. She hadn't felt this bedraggled since her older brother had accidentally pushed her into a mud puddle when she'd been in sixth grade.

Kyle was waiting for her when she entered the apartment. He was sitting in his recliner with a lapful of blueprints and papers.

"Surprise. Lunch is all ready—" He paused as he looked up and saw her for the first time. "What happened to you?"

"I got wet." Victoria kicked off her shoes and stripped off her raincoat. Her dress was worse off than she'd thought. She'd have to change, she couldn't go back to work this way. "Some idiot ran a red light and I got splashed."

"Go put on some dry clothes," Kyle instructed her, as if she hadn't thought of it herself. "Then come back and have some stew. I warmed it up in the microwave for you."

"You're not supposed to be doing that yet."

"No problem. Everything's under control." He made no mention of the two glasses he'd broken in the sink while preparing lunch. Some things were better left unsaid. "Go on, go change out of those wet clothes."

Victoria was passing the phone in the hall when it rang. "Hello?"

"Is Kyle there?" a woman asked in a husky drawl.

"Yes, just a minute." She carried the cordless receiver over to Kyle. "It's for you."

"Hello? Angelica? What a surprise. You're where? Wait a second—! Hello?" Kyle swore and slammed the receiver down on a nearby end table. "She was calling from her limo. It's downstairs. She's on her way up now."

"Now?" Victoria looked down at her wet clothes in dismay. "She can't come now. I'm not ready."

"I'll have Bernie stall her." Kyle called the doorman and left instructions. "Don't let anyone up for ten—no, make that fifteen minutes, Bernie."

Victoria raced down the hallway, already unbuttoning the cuffs on her sleeves. She tore off her dress as soon as she closed the bedroom door. Her wet panty hose came next, but not without a struggle. Two broken nails later, she finally peeled them off and threw them in the trash.

What to wear, what to wear? Her mind went blank as she yanked open her closet door. Then she heard the sound of the front door buzzer.

Apparently Angelica wasn't easy to stall.

Victoria could hear the muffled sound of Kyle swearing. She repeated a few of the phrases herself.

"Are you dressed yet?" he yelled down the hall.

"No!"

The door buzzer sounded again.

"Tory, hurry up! Just throw something on and get out here," he told her.

"Easy for you to say," she muttered.

The buzzer was now accompanied by impatient knocking.

"I'm coming," Kyle shouted. "Hold on a second." Grabbing his crutches, he hobbled to the door and flung it open.

The moment Angelica stepped over the threshold, she pasted herself to him, almost knocking him over with the gesture.

"Oh, you poor darling!" she cooed.

Kyle had a hard time disentangling himself from her clinging embrace. He would have had more trouble if Angelica hadn't suddenly released him and demanded, "Who's that?"

He looked over his shoulder, relieved at Tory's prompt appearance. His relief turned to shock when he saw what she was wearing. He supposed it could be called a robe, but it wasn't like any robe he'd ever seen her wear before. In fact, it wasn't like *anything* he'd ever seen her wear, period! The slinky black material lovingly hugged her curves and the black lace trim contrasted strikingly with her pale skin. She made an enticing picture, classy yet very, very sexy.

Mustering her courage, Victoria walked right up to Kyle and put her arm through his. "Do introduce me."

It was all false bravado on her part. Seeing Angelica in Kyle's arms had brought out her protective instincts. She was also experiencing a wave of jealousy—and depression.

Angelica looked the way she sounded. Sultry. In fact, she reminded Victoria of Susan Lucci, the sexy daytime actress who was so good at being bad. Angelica's hair was long and dark, and her makeup was flawless. Dressed in a fur coat and flashing a huge diamond ring, she oozed wealth.

"Yes, Kyle," Angelica said in a husky drawl. "Do introduce me to your little friend."

Since Victoria topped Angelica by at least three inches, she thought it rather amusing to be referred to as "little." *You're either regaining your sense of humor,* she told herself, *or you're becoming hysterical.*

"Angelica Van Horne, this is Victoria Winters. Darling, this is Mrs. Van Horne."

Not only was Victoria startled to hear Kyle calling her *darling*, she was also surprised when he draped his arm around her shoulders in a move that was clearly possessive. He'd never touched her that way before—seriously, as if he really meant it. This was no teasing gesture of friendship. She could feel the warmth of his hand right through the thin material of her robe. Her skin actually tingled as he rubbed his thumb across the rounded tip of her shoulder. The absentminded caress threw her. So did the way she liked it. She wasn't supposed to be enjoying the situation this much.

Striving to regain her perspective, she turned toward their guest with a politeness she didn't feel. "Mrs. Van Horne, I'm so glad to meet you at last. Kyle has told me so much about you."

"Funny," Angelica retorted, "he hasn't told me a thing about you."

Victoria shrugged off the news with unperturbed confidence. "Isn't that just like a man? They never talk about what's important in their lives."

"Well, Kyle, aren't you going to invite me in?" Angelica didn't wait for an answer. She sauntered into the living room with a walk that a model would have envied. Even the way she sat down on a chair was poised.

Victoria felt decidedly underdressed in her robe and bare feet. Kyle gave her the courage to go on. He wasn't watching Angelica, he was watching her. She couldn't let him down.

Drawing in a deep breath, she prepared herself for round two. "Welcome to our humble abode, and make yourself at home," Victoria drawled with mocking humor.

Angelica's composure slipped. "You mean you live here, too?"

"That's right," Victoria replied cheerfully as she followed Kyle into the living room.

Wanting this incident to be over as soon as possible, Kyle cautiously lowered himself to the couch and tugged Victoria down beside him. Victoria seemed to be handling herself just fine, but he didn't want this turning into a free-for-all. Angelica was a barracuda, and he didn't want her taking any bites out of Tory.

"It was nice of you to be concerned, Angelica, but as you can see, Tory is taking very good care of me." To emphasize his claim, Kyle moved his hand from the back of the couch to Victoria's waist.

Victoria almost jumped out of her skin as he began brushing his fingers up and down her spine. She should have put on something more substantial, she frantically thought to herself. She'd never worn anything this revealing in front of Kyle before. And she'd never felt this edge of excitement with him before, either.

Angelica watched them closely. "I must say I'm a little surprised, Kyle. Judging from your behavior, I'd always assumed that you were unattached."

Victoria's eyes narrowed suspiciously at that. Just what kind of behavior was Angelica referring to? she wondered.

"You assumed wrong," was all Kyle said.

"Really?" Angelica did not look convinced. "Tell me, have you two known each other long, Kyle?"

"Yes."

"I see... how long?"

Kyle stuck to monosyllabic answers. "Years."

"You've been dating each other for years?"

"No."

"I don't understand. How long *have* you two been dating each other?"

Wanting to help him out of a tough spot, Victoria jumped into the fray. She and Kyle answered simultaneously. Unfortunately, they didn't answer identically.

"Eight months," he said.

"Two years," she said.

Angelica raised her perfectly penciled eyebrows.

Kyle gave Victoria's shoulder a slight squeeze, cautioning her to let him answer. "Actually, we've been seeing each other for two years, but it's become much more serious in the past eight months."

"Where did you two lovebirds meet?" Her question was edged with sarcasm.

"Right here in New York City," Victoria answered, figuring she couldn't go wrong with that reply.

"Fancy that. Kyle and I found each other here in New York City, too." Angelica launched into a long, involved story about how she and Kyle had first met. "How long have you two been living together, Victoria?" she suddenly inserted.

"Eighteen months," Victoria answered, deciding it was safest to stick to the truth as much as possible.

"Really? How interesting. You've only been seeing each other seriously for eight months, yet you moved in here with Kyle eighteen months ago."

Kyle quickly recovered the fumble. "Did I say eight months? I meant eighteen. An easy mistake."

"So you've been serious about each other for eighteen months. Strange. Eighteen months ago Kyle took over as one of our troubleshooters in the international division. He hasn't been home much since then."

Sensing that Victoria was about to respond, Kyle brushed the back of his hand against her cheek, effectively silencing her.

"It's not the quantity of time that counts, it's the quality," he said.

"You don't mind all the traveling he does?" Angelica's question was again directed at Victoria.

"Not at all."

Kyle's frown made her realize that maybe she shouldn't have sounded quite so cheerful about his absences. "I mean, of course I miss him, but I know he's coming back." That didn't sound much better, she decided with chagrin.

Kyle apparently agreed. Pulling her close, he nuzzled her earlobe. "Just keep quiet and let me do all the talking," he growled softly.

The feel of his lips brushing across her skin made her shiver. She told herself to stay calm, that her reaction was caused by a chill in the air. Or maybe the stress of the moment. Certainly nothing more. She was determined to keep her feet on the ground. Besides, he had no business ordering her around when she was doing him a favor.

"Kyle says the sweetest things," she murmured for Angelica's benefit.

"I know he does," Angelica murmured right back.

Deciding it was time he took control of the situation, Kyle unequivocally stated, "Nobody knows me as well as Tory does." And with something of a shock, he realized he was telling the truth. There weren't many people he'd trust guarding his back, but he'd trust her.

"I think you're underestimating me," Angelica declared. "I know you better than you think, Kyle."

No, you don't, but you'd like to, Victoria thought to herself. *Well, forget it, Madame Man-eater. There's no way I'm letting you get your crimson claws into Kyle.*

Unfortunately, her time for this little gathering was quickly running out. She had a job to get back to. Grabbing hold of Kyle's hand, she squinted at his wristwatch. She could have looked at her own, but it wouldn't have been as intimate. And it undoubtedly wouldn't have left her heart beating this fast, she admitted. "Oh, my gosh, look at the time. It's getting late. I've got to get back to work."

"Is that what you usually wear to work?" Angelica asked with a catty smile.

Hey, two can play that game, lady. Victoria took great pleasure in saying, "No, this is what I wear to play." A sultry look at Kyle got her message across very succinctly.

Foreseeing imminent fireworks, Kyle hastened to add, "I'm sure you've got a busy schedule, too, Angelica, so we won't keep you."

"I'll be in touch," Angelica promised before leaving.

"You touch and I'll chop your hand off," the normally peace-loving Victoria muttered as the other woman left.

She was still muttering as she walked out of her apartment building to return to work. She was going to be late.

Angelica made sure she was even later. "Where are you going?" she inquired through the open tinted-glass window of her limo. "I'll give you a lift."

"No, thanks." Victoria kept walking. "I don't work far from here."

Angelica gave a sign to the chauffeur, who matched the car's progress to Victoria's. "Oh, do you work in one of those cute little bars down on First Avenue?"

"No, I work at the UN." Having said that, Victoria made the most of a break in the traffic and dashed across the street.

Angelica sat back with a satisfied smile as she activated the power window, effectively blocking out the mayhem of the city. "So she works for the UN, does she? We'll just have to see about that."

Four

When she got back to the office, Victoria had a hard time explaining her tardiness to her boss. Walter Molenaar was punctual to a fault and had standards higher than the World Trade Center. As an international civil servant bucking for a higher-level professional posting, he didn't allow anything or anyone to slip past him.

She knew she was in for a lecture when he called her into his office. Mr. Molenaar reprimanded her in a well-modulated voice that held the hint of an accent from his native Belgium. He waved aside Victoria's attempts to blame the weather. "If you hadn't left the building and gone home for lunch you would not have gotten wet and you would not have been late." His pronouncement had a familiar I-told-you-so ring to it. "See that it doesn't happen again."

As if Victoria didn't have enough problems, a new group from the Egyptian mission needed their papers processed before the end of the day. Most of the protocol department's work involved clearing paperwork for the seven thousand UN employees, who were from more than 140 countries. It was difficult keeping track of the comings and goings of so many people, from so many countries, with so many varying visa and immunization requirements. Some days it felt as though all seven thousand of them wanted their demands met at the same time. Today was one of those days. She stayed late to make up for the time she'd lost at lunch.

When she finally did get home, Kyle was playing the blues on his harmonica. She hadn't realized how good he'd gotten. He'd obviously been practicing while he'd been away. Still, he stopped playing when he realized she was home.

"You didn't have to stop," she said. "Your playing doesn't bother me."

Kyle knew that. Nothing bothered Tory. But a lot of things were bothering him lately, things he couldn't even put a name to, things he didn't want to think about.

He set his harmonica aside and said, "You look tired. Let's order a pizza for dinner."

"Sounds good to me." Victoria hadn't relished the prospect of cooking dinner after such a stressful day.

Later, as they munched on a pepperoni, black olive and mushroom pizza, Victoria gave her assessment of the meeting with Angelica.

"She wasn't convinced. Our performance needs improving."

"What would you suggest?" Kyle asked.

"I don't know. What do you think?"

"I think we should go out on a real date," he said. "That way we can at least refer back to an actual occurrence instead of making stuff up as we go along. There's less chance for making the mistakes we made today."

"I thought we did pretty well, considering we had no warning."

Kyle shrugged noncommittally. "Where did you get that thing you were wearing?" he asked in a deliberately casual voice.

"Which thing?"

"That slinky thing you wore when Angelica was here."

"I got it out of my closet."

"I haven't seen it before."

Now it was her turn to shrug.

Kyle pressed on. "Did you buy it for yourself?"

"Well, I certainly didn't buy it for my great-aunt Sophie," she drawled with a mocking grin.

"So you did buy it for yourself?"

"Kyle, why are you asking me all these questions?"

"No reason."

She wondered. Wondered about all sorts of things she probably shouldn't have. Wondered what Kyle had thought about her appearance, what he was thinking now. Had he liked what he'd seen? Did she want him to? So many questions, so few answers.

Noticing the way he was staring at her so intently, she added another question to her list: did she have tomato sauce on her face? She wiped a paper napkin across her mouth and dabbed surreptitiously at her chin. No tomato sauce. No trace of lipstick, either. That came as no surprise, but she felt disappointed, nonetheless. The new lipstick she'd been wearing was supposed to be "extra long-lasting." But apparently it couldn't withstand her nervous habit of biting her lips when she was under pressure. Great. She probably looked like a washed-out ghost. It shouldn't have mattered, but it did. She didn't want to look bad in front of Kyle.

And that was not a good sign. She knew that, but knowing it with her rational mind and knowing it with her recalcitrant heart were two different things. She told herself there was nothing to worry about. That she had everything under control. That she didn't really care if Kyle saw her with or without lipstick.

Keeping that in mind, she took another slice of pizza. Eating made her feel better, which was why she'd been fifteen pounds overweight when she'd first met Kyle.

Kyle watched her bite into the pizza with dainty white teeth. He watched her lick the tomato sauce off her lips. He was watching her too damn much. This was Tory. He'd seen her eat pizza plenty of times. He even knew *how* she ate it—she always picked the black olives off the top first. The image erased the brief mental flash he'd had of her in that slinky robe. He found the link between Tory and black olives much more comforting than the link between her and black satin.

Reassured, he said, "So where do you think we should go for this official date of ours?"

"Where would you take me if we really were going out together?"

"That depends."

"On what?" she asked.

"On how long I'd known you. If it was a first date and I didn't know you very well, I'd probably take you out to dinner. If I knew you as well as I know you now, then I'd know how much you like roller-skating, and I might take you to a rink."

"I'm not sure going roller-skating on a date would convince Angelica of our romantic involvement."

"You're probably right," he agreed. "Okay, scratch that. How about dinner and a show?"

She shook her head. "Too normal."

"Okay, then *you* think of something."

"It should be something romantic." She closed her eyes dreamily. "You know, moonlight and roses, dancing under the stars." She came back to earth with a grin. Looking at his cast, she said, "Sorry. Dancing is out," and then ducked when he threw a crumpled-up paper napkin at her. "I've got it!" She snapped her fingers. "How about dinner and a buggy ride around Central Park? That way I still get a meal out and we do something romantic, killing two birds with one stone."

"What makes you think a buggy ride around Central Park is romantic? I thought it was touristy."

"Trust me, it's romantic."

"Are you speaking from personal experience here, or what?" The idea disturbed him for some reason.

"No, although I've always wanted to, I've never been on a buggy ride."

"Well, if you say it's romantic, I'll take your word for it. When should we go? Tomorrow night?"

"I think that's a little soon for you to be out gallivanting around on that ankle of yours. You only flew in from Cairo five days ago, Kyle. Don't rush it. Besides, uh, I've already got a date tomorrow night."

"Anybody I know?"

Victoria shook her head. "Nobody I even know. Sue set it up. We're double-dating two guys from the office where she works." Sue worked for the American subsidiary of a major European conglomerate.

"A blind date?" Kyle looked disapproving. "That doesn't sound very safe to me, Tory."

"It's a double date. I won't be alone. And Sue knows them both. She works with them every day."

"Just be glad I'll be here to check this guy out when he picks you up."

"Actually, he's not picking me up, I'm meeting them all at a restaurant. So you see, I'm already being cautious. I'm not having any strange men come to the apartment. That should make you feel better. I know how you worry about strangers coming in and tampering with your rock collection." Kyle had an extensive collection of geodes he'd gathered on his travels around the world, and Victoria loved teasing him about his attachment to them.

"It's not my rock collection I'm worried about."

"Your etchings, then?"

"No. I'm worried about you."

"There's no need to be. I'll be fine, you'll see."

She might have been fine, but her date wasn't. He was another up-and-comer on the ladder of success, and he spent all his time telling her how bright, talented and important he was. Actually, Victoria was glad that she didn't have to participate in a two-way conversation. It gave her a chance to mull over Kyle's unexpected reaction to her going out tonight. It was probably nothing more than his protective instincts coming to the fore, but it made her wonder how it would feel to have Kyle actually be jealous over her. *Dream on,* she told herself. And she did.

Her date never noticed that she was off in another world. He just kept talking.

Sue's date wasn't going much better. Both women were eager to make it an early night. They insisted that the men needn't bother seeing them home and hurriedly hailed a cab.

Once they were on their way, Victoria looked at Sue, Sue looked at her, and they both started laughing.

"Sorry about that. They seemed normal enough at work," Sue said between giggles.

"I definitely heard more than I ever wanted to know about Roger Leibman and every vacation he's taken in the past five years," Victoria stated. "How about you? How was your date? He seemed to be doing an awful lot of talking."

"It was all work. We talked about business the whole time. He's working on a new project, and he wanted my opinion on it."

"Trying to pick your brain for brilliant ideas, hmmm?"

"Yes. And probably planning on taking all the credit himself, if I'd given him one. I'm sorry the night was such a disaster."

"It wasn't a total loss," Victoria pointed out. "The dinner was good."

"Good but tiny. The portions they give you in that place are microscopic. What do you say we check out that new all-night ice-cream emporium near you?"

"Sounds good to me."

The light in Kyle's room was still on when Victoria tiptoed down the hallway a little after midnight.

"How was your date?" he asked.

"We didn't have much in common," she admitted.

"Too bad."

"Yeah." She took a few steps into his room. "So what did you do all evening?"

"Caught up on my paperwork."

"How's your ankle doing?"

He grunted, which Victoria took to mean that it hurt. "Try elevating it. Sue said that helped when she broke her leg." She picked up one of the studio couch pillows from the floor and carried it to the bed. Then she lifted Kyle's ankle, raising it more than she'd meant to. Her action threw him off balance, and he fell backward. The papers he'd been working on scattered all over the floor, and Victoria ended up sprawled across his bare chest.

"I'm not sure that *really* helped, Tory," he drawled.

Victoria lay there for a moment, frozen. Her cheek was resting on the warmth of his skin, and the sound of his voice rumbled in her ear. She could feel his heart beating steadily, slowly. Unlike hers, which was pounding like a wild thing.

"Sorry," she muttered, and scrambled to her feet. "I guess that wasn't such a good idea. Let me get these papers back together for you."

His normally unperturbed Tory was actually blushing, Kyle realized in amazement. Because of him? Or because of something that had happened on that damn blind date of hers? Had she been daydreaming about that other guy, the one she didn't have much in common with, when she'd been lifting his ankle? Was that why she hadn't paid attention to what she was doing?

Whoa, slow down, O'Reilly, he told himself. He was jumping to unfounded conclusions, he knew that. Tory wasn't the daydreaming type. She was probably blushing because she felt silly losing her balance the way she had.

"You know we never did settle on a day for our official date," he said as she gathered up the last of the papers. "What about next Friday night? That gives me all week to perfect my crutch-walking routine."

"Friday's fine."

"Good. Friday it is, then."

"Okay. I'll just leave these papers on the table here. Good night." She hurried from the room before she could make a bigger fool of herself.

Victoria blamed her blush on embarrassment and didn't delve any further than that. Ditto for her racing heart. She'd been embarrassed at falling all over Kyle. And surprised. A natural reaction. It had nothing to do with attraction. It had been shock, that was all. She refused to brood about it.

As the week went on, the incident gradually faded from her mind. There were plenty of other things to distract her, most of them at work. Badly needing a break, she did manage to slip out and come home for lunch once.

Kyle was watching television when she walked in. Noticing the way he quickly turned it off, she suspected he'd been watching a soap opera. "What was it? *Days of Our Lives* or *All My Children*?"

"It was a documentary on oil extraction in the North Sea," he claimed. "On PBS."

Victoria smiled, recognizing defensiveness when she heard it. "Sounds fascinating," she said. "Turn it back on, we'll both watch it."

"It just finished."

She switched the TV back on. "Then you won't mind if we turn on my favorite soap." Sure enough, the channel was not set on public television. "Aha, caught with your hand in the soap opera jar!"

"I thought you told me they were supposed to be called daytime dramas."

"You're absolutely right. So fill me in on what's happened on this daytime drama so far today," she requested as she went into the kitchen to fix a quick lunch.

With a reluctant grin, Kyle gave a short synopsis.

"How's the practice going with your crutches?" she asked when the show was over and they'd eaten their ham sandwiches and corn chips.

"Progressing by leaps and bounds."

"Sounds pretty strenuous to me."

"All right, I'm not leaping yet. But I'll be ready for our date on Friday, never fear. Believe me, being stuck here is no picnic."

"Gee, thanks a lot," she said with a huffiness that was only partially affected. "Maybe you would have preferred being stuck in Cairo?"

"You know what I mean. I'm getting cabin fever."

The only time Kyle had gotten out was when he'd ridden the elevator down to the lobby and played a game of poker with Bernie, the doorman. They were scheduled for another game later that afternoon.

"Anyone ever tell you that you play a mean game of poker, Mr. O'Reilly?"

"Call me Kyle, Bernie, and you're not so bad yourself."

"Don't see as much of you as I used to," Bernie noted as he shuffled the cards for another hand.

"I do a lot of traveling."

"So I hear. It may not be my place to say, but Mr. Dinkman's got his eyes on you and Miss Winters. I've told him you're both good tenants, but he doesn't listen to me. What do I know?" Bernie grumbled. "I've only been the doorman here for ten years. Mr. Big Shot's been here a measly two years. You know, he only got the job of building manager because his wife is one of the owner's cousins."

"Ah, the fiery de Franco brothers. They're still split about converting the building to condos, aren't they?"

"That's right," Bernie said.

"Good." Kyle knew that a lot of the buildings in this area had already gone condo, but so far his apartment was safe. Though he earned a comfortable living, he didn't want to have to make a sizable investment to keep a place he rarely used.

The story was that the two de Franco brothers had had a fraternal feud going for years. They never agreed on anything, including the building's future. One brother wanted to convert the building to condominiums, but so far the other one had refused to go along with the trend. Kyle hoped the stalemate would continue, but both men were in their late sixties, and it was only a matter of time before a change would come, one way or another. It wasn't something he liked thinking about.

"Don't worry about the building going condo," Bernie advised him. "Worry about Mr. Dinkman. I think he's hoping to prove himself to the de Francos so they'll promote him again."

"Thanks for the warning, Bernie."

"You and Miss Winter are a nice couple. I'd hate to see you leave."

Kyle found it strangely disturbing to hear himself and Tory referred to as a couple. Sure, that was the smoke screen they'd put up for Dinkman and now for Angelica. But for some reason hearing Bernie call them "a nice couple" upset him. Tory represented friendship, and the word "couple" represented something sexual. And, in his mind, the two didn't mix. At least they never had in the past.

Tory was a great friend, one of the few people he could really talk to. She always seemed to know when he wanted to be alone and when he needed company. They were comfortable with each other, and that had taken years to achieve. With all the changes going on in the rest of his life, he didn't want things between himself and Tory to change. She was the one thing that remained stable—whether he was in Egypt, Brazil or Taiwan, Tory was his anchor.

Yet he couldn't deny noticing how sexy she'd looked in that slinky black robe. After all, he was human. But he'd seen the hell Liz and Jeff had put themselves through when they'd tried mixing friendship with romance. With that kind of example to go by, he didn't think he and Tory would have any trouble abstaining. They were both smart enough to steer clear of dangerous undercurrents.

By the time Friday rolled around, Kyle was really looking forward to going out. His broken ankle had caused more complications than he'd expected. Getting dressed had been an exercise in frustration until he'd sent several pairs of slacks to a tailor for a few alterations on the right pant leg seams. At least now he could put his pants on over the cast. It had gotten rather chilly running around the apartment in a pair of shorts in October. In addition to being able to wear long pants again, Kyle was feeling more confident about his ability to get around with the crutches.

Still, it did feel a little strange going through the ritual of getting ready for a date, knowing that he was going out with Tory. He wondered if she was feeling nervous, too, and then dismissed the idea. Tory never got nervous. She was always calm and soothing. Except when he'd burst in on her in the tub. His mind flashed back to the image of her sitting there covered with all those bubbles. He wondered when she'd outgrown the baby fat she'd had in college. Why hadn't he noticed how pretty she'd become? He wondered how much longer it would be before some guy snatched her up and married her.

Kyle swore and tied his tie for the fifth time.

In her room, Victoria was trying on the third outfit she'd pulled out of her closet. The first had been too casual, the second too dressy. She didn't want Kyle to think she was dressing up for him, trying to get his attention. Yet she wanted to look good.

"This is ridiculous!" she muttered to herself. "It's only Kyle you're going out with, not Tom Cruise. Calm down and get dressed. Otherwise you're going to be late for dinner."

She settled on a jersey dress in teal blue that always made her feel good. The skirt flared at the waist and made her look slim. She kept her jewelry and makeup simple yet classy. Brown eye pencil and mascara accented the soft taupe shadow she'd applied to her eyelids. The effect emphasized her unusual coloring—brown eyes and blond hair. She'd partially tamed her wavy shoulder-length hair with gold hair clasps that matched her gold earrings and necklace.

Taking a deep breath, she slipped on her shoes and aimed a spritz of Vanderbilt perfume at each wrist. She was ready.

Kyle and Victoria opened their respective bedroom doors at the same time. They looked at each other and were momentarily tongue-tied. It was as if two strangers were standing there, eyeing each other, sizing each other up, trying to read one another's minds.

Victoria looked into Kyle's blue eyes with unaccustomed shyness. She was surprised to see a nervousness there that almost matched her own. Finally recognizing their mutual state of anxiety, they both smiled.

"You look real nice," Kyle told her.

"Thanks. So do you."

"Crutches and all?"

"Crutches and all," she said, and she wasn't just being polite. He looked great. He wore dark slacks and an ice-blue shirt. Her discerning eyes noted that his jacket and tie both had tiny flecks of ice blue mixed in with the otherwise somber charcoal-gray wool.

"If you're all set, let's blow this pop stand. After you." He motioned her ahead with a courtly bow that was at odds with the jargon he'd used.

They were both quiet on the short elevator ride down to the lobby. They looked at each other, smiled and then looked away, only to look at each other again. It really was beginning to feel like a bona fide date.

Even though it was a Friday night, Bernie got them a cab right away. "You two have a nice evening, now," he said as he waved them off.

The restaurant, one of the city's more recently opened establishments, was just around the corner from the Plaza Hotel. It was discreetly romantic. The soft lighting came from crystal chandeliers. Victoria noticed and admired the ultraplush carpeting, damask tablecloths, delicate bone china and fresh-cut flowers. But after they were seated, she noticed something else.

"Kyle, there aren't any prices on my menu."

"That's right." He looked at her over the top of the oversize menu. "Order whatever you'd like. We're celebrating tonight."

"What are we celebrating?"

"The fact that I can get around again. It feels good to be out."

She wondered if he'd been bored staying at home with her. "You make it sound like you just got out of prison...."

Her voice trailed off as she realized that the busboy pouring their water had overheard her last few words.

After the nervous young man had made a hurried exit Kyle couldn't resist teasing her. "Nice going, Tory. Now the hired help thinks I'm an ex-con."

She grinned. "He did look sort of startled, didn't he?"

"I thought he was going to spill that pitcher full of ice water in my lap."

"A refreshing way to begin the evening, I'm sure."

"We're not looking for *refreshing*, we're looking for *romantic*, remember?"

"Got it." This was the sort of friendly banter she felt comfortable with.

"Now, since your French is better than mine, why don't you translate the menu for me." Kyle's French was adequate, but he enjoyed hearing Tory speak the language. "I recognize most of these, but a few of them have got me stymied. I know *petits filets de boeuf aux champignons* is filet mignon with mushrooms, but what is *côtelletes d'agneau à l'estragon*?"

"Lamb with tarragon sauce." Victoria went through the rest of the menu with him, translating the occasional item that was somewhat out of the ordinary.

"Okay, what are you going to order?" he asked.

"What are you having?"

"The filet mignon. And you?"

As Victoria answered him in French, Kyle noticed how the words rolled off her tongue. The language was suited to her voice, which was low and husky. He'd forgotten how sexy it made her sound. When she spoke French she seemed more mysterious to him, more sophisticated—and that threw him.

He used humor in an attempt to regain his equilibrium. "Sounds great. Somehow veal cooked in apple cider just doesn't have the same ring to it."

"I'm more interested in how it tastes than how it sounds."

He smiled as her comment transformed the continental lady back into his longtime pal. "Ah, the ever-practical Tory."

"Speaking of being practical, are you sure this isn't too expensive for you—"

He cut her off. "Would you stop worrying about money? I'm still getting paid while I'm on this medical leave, so there's nothing to worry about. Sit back, relax, and enjoy it."

That was easy to do. Their food was delicious, their surroundings elegant. Victoria sampled some of his steak and gave him a taste of her veal. For dessert they both had passion fruit sorbet.

Kyle didn't even blink when he was presented with what must have been a very expensive bill, if the generous tip he left was any gauge.

"Stop frowning, it'll give you wrinkles," Kyle said once they were outside. "The dinner was worth it. I enjoyed it. Didn't you?"

She nodded.

"Good. Then let's move on to the second part of our evening—the carriage ride." A number of carriages were lined up along the park, which was just across the street. Kyle put two fingers in his mouth and whistled loud enough to get a driver's attention.

"How's your ankle holding up?" she asked him as the carriage driver began maneuvering his way across the lanes of traffic.

"It's the cast and the crutches that are holding me up, not the ankle. I'm doing fine."

Still, Victoria worried about having him climb into the carriage. She hadn't taken his broken ankle into consideration when she'd first suggested that they take a buggy ride.

As it turned out, Kyle managed fine. He was able to climb into the back of the buggy without falling flat on his face. It might not have been particularly graceful, but it was successful.

"Hey, you did that pretty well," she told him.

"If you think that was good, you should see my swan dive."

"I've seen your swan dive."

"So you have." Kyle shifted, hoping for a more comfortable position.

His shoulder brushed against hers, and Victoria shivered.

"Are you cold? Here, cover up with this." He unfolded a tartan blanket from the corner of the seat and tucked it around her. Then he joined her underneath it.

They sat side by side, so close together that she could feel his body heat. She felt flustered and thrilled, nervous and pleased—all the contradicting emotions that spelled attraction. She immediately corrected herself. Not attraction. What then? Enjoyment? Yes, that sounded better.

"It's too bad it's dark. It would have been nice to see the fall colors in the park," she said for lack of anything else to say. Could he tell she was babbling?

"I don't know, being in the dark has its advantages." He put his arm around her to prevent them from bumping into each other as the carriage bounced along. "It's more romantic this way, isn't it?"

She didn't know if he was referring to the darkness or to his embrace, but her answer was the same for both. "Yes, it is."

Their conversation lagged even more after that as they became engrossed in their own thoughts.

Victoria couldn't remember an evening she'd enjoyed more. In fact, she was probably enjoying herself more than she should. She knew she'd gotten caught up in the charade, but she couldn't seem to help it. As the carriage ride progressed, so, too, did her fantasies. She imagined that this was a real date, that she and Kyle had just met. It was love at first sight. After a wonderfully romantic dinner, he'd suggested a ride around the park and she'd accepted. They were snuggled together, cocooned in a world of darkness. She closed her eyes and dreamed on.

"Thanks."

The sound of Kyle's voice so close to her ear startled her, and she jumped guiltily. Her eyes flew open. "Wh-what?"

"I said thanks."

"For what?" She turned her head sharply. Her action brought them almost nose-to-nose.

They both froze. Something was happening between them, something that had nothing to do with friendship. A sensual awareness had suddenly sprung up, electrifying the very air around them. The world slipped away as they stared at each other, their breaths mingling, their lips almost touching.

"Thanks for... helping me... celebrate." Kyle spoke the words as if they were in a foreign language.

Her reply was equally breathless. "Oh... you're... welcome...."

His kiss, which he told himself had been intended for her cheek, landed instead on her parted lips. Neither of them turned away. As if their bodies recognized something their minds didn't, their mouths blended together in perfect accord.

Victoria closed her eyes and let the magic carry her away. This wasn't real. It was all part of her dream. The real Kyle would never be kissing her so passionately. And this kiss was passionate, intensely so. But then it was over as suddenly as it had begun.

"Hey, the ride's over, folks!" the driver announced with a cheerful laugh.

Kyle and Victoria sprang apart like a pair of guilty teenagers.

Victoria looked at Kyle in wide-eyed dismay. The ride might be over, she thought to herself, but the trouble was just beginning!

Five

Victoria's way of coping with the confusing aftermath of Kyle's kiss was to ignore it. Pretend it had never happened. Wipe it from her memory. She'd taken her cue from Kyle, and when he'd acted as if nothing had happened, so had she. Throughout that night and the next few days, neither one of them had made any reference to their kiss or to the bewildering emotions it had provoked.

Instead, they both doggedly stuck to their normal routine of friendship as if it were the only stable thing left in a world turned upside down. Each played the part of buddy to the hilt. They joked and laughed together, the way they always did. They teased each other, the way they always did. But without being overly obvious about it, they'd begun to avoid touching each other.

Victoria was more aware of the subtle difference than Kyle was. This already difficult time for her was made even worse by the fact that the person in whom she normally confided her troubles was now the very same person who was causing those troubles—Kyle. All she could do was keep pretending that nothing had changed and hope that this temporary awkwardness would abate.

By the end of the weekend, Kyle and Victoria had both managed to convince themselves that they'd forgotten all about their kiss. It was a case of willing themselves back to normal. The endeavor took all of their energy, but it was so successful that neither one guessed the other was only acting.

On Tuesday Kyle had to venture out again to keep a doctor's appointment. He was relieved to hear that his ankle was healing right on schedule. But it would still be another two or three weeks before he'd be given a walking cast. Until then he had to continue using the crutches. The trip left him feeling restless and impatient. The cab rides to and from the doctor's office were a chore. He almost poked his eye out with his crutch when he got into the last dilapidated taxi. New York City was not an easy place to negotiate on crutches, and that realization frustrated him.

Victoria refused to let him get discouraged. She gave him all the encouragement a man could ask for, and then some—he realized that. She didn't take his moods to heart. When he got out of hand, she let him know by cheerfully threatening to break his other ankle if he yelled at her again.

Still, there were times, when she didn't think he was watching her, that she became quiet and her brown eyes looked sad. The moment she caught him looking at her, she put on a bright face. Sometimes Kyle got the impression that she was deliberately hiding something from him.

The idea hurt him. Tory had always confided in him in the past, and he'd taken it for granted that she always would in the future.

Right now she was curled up on the living room couch, her legs tucked under her in her favorite pose. As he sat in his recliner, Kyle observed the way she frowned at the letter from her parents that she was reading.

"Something wrong?" he asked her.

"No. My younger brother added a postscript, and I was just trying to decipher his handwriting. I swear they must give medical students a course in illegible handwriting when they enter school." She folded the letter and stuck it back in the envelope. "I think his cryptic message had something to do with a charity costume party at the teaching hospital."

"Speaking of costume parties, George's annual Halloween bash is this weekend," Kyle reminded her.

"Oh, my gosh! I'd almost forgotten about that."

"You're planning on going, aren't you?" He sounded worried.

"Of course I'm going," she assured him breezily. "Why wouldn't I?"

"No reason."

They looked at each and then quickly looked away.

Kyle cleared his throat. "At least no one will have any trouble identifying me this year, not with this cast on my ankle."

"I don't know." She eyed him thoughtfully. "It depends what kind of costume we come up with for you."

"We?"

"Well, we're a team, aren't we?"

Kyle nodded. He was glad to hear Tory sounding like her old self again. "That's right, we're a team."

"Then let's see what we can come up with."

"Have you decided what you're going to wear yet?" he asked.

Victoria shook her head.

Kyle thought of something right away. "Florence Nightingale. It's perfect for you, Tory."

A cap and white nursing shoes. Lovely. Victoria preferred to concentrate on his costume rather than her own. "What about you?"

"I could go as a wounded hero. You know, put my arm in a sling and pour ketchup on it," Kyle said.

"I think that's what you wore the last time you went to one of George's costume parties. When was that?" She tried to remember. "You weren't in town for Halloween last year, so it must have been the year before. No, we've got to come up with something different this time."

"Why? I liked the wounded hero idea."

Victoria smiled as inspiration struck. "Forget the wounded hero, I've got a better idea!"

"I told you no one would recognize you," she murmured to Kyle as they stood in a room crowded with Frankensteins and Statues of Liberty. "It's the perfect costume."

"You wouldn't think so if you were wrapped up in all this stuff. It's hot in here," he growled. "And my right ear itches."

"Mummies aren't supposed to itch."

She could see his blue eyes glaring at her through the narrow slits left in the white material that covered him from head to toe. "Okay, already." She reached out and scratched his ear, or at least where she thought his ear might be. "Is that better?"

He nodded. "I can't believe I let you talk me into this."

"I think the crutches are the perfect touch."

"I never saw a mummy on crutches in any of those old horror movies."

"At least you're unique," she retorted. "I've already seen three wounded warriors walk by, and we just got here."

"I think you just wanted to wrap me up as punishment for ordering that Florence Nightingale costume for you."

"You should have checked with me first, Kyle."

"It looks nice on you."

She grimaced. *Nice? Swell.*

"Aren't you warm with that cloak on?" he asked her.

"Uh, no, I'm fine." She didn't tell him that the costume was someone's idea of a joke, because underneath the demure navy blue cloak was a bodice that looked as though it had been spray painted on her! If this was a size ten, she'd eat her nurse's cap. "Shall we mingle?"

"You mingle. I'm going to go sit over there with George, alias Pee Wee Herman."

"Tell him I said the hairdo and the jacket look good on him."

Kyle nodded and took off with an ambling swing of his crutches.

Victoria was standing by the refreshment table when Sue came up to her. "Florence Nightingale? Let me guess. Kyle's idea?"

She nodded. "You look great, Sue. That saloon-girl costume looks like something right out of *Gunsmoke*."

"Thanks. What do you think of George's imitation of Pee Wee Herman?"

"It's better than Jeff's imitation of Superman."

"You think so?" Sue sounded doubtful. "Hey, check out the cowboy over there. Looks good. Never mind, he's with Minnie Mouse."

"I can't believe George got this many adults to dress up in ridiculous costumes and come here tonight," Victoria said. "I mean, when we were all in college it was one thing, but most of these people are well past the student-prankster stage."

"We're all just kids at heart, I guess."

"Who are all these people?" Victoria asked. "I don't think I know more than a handful."

"Judging from last year's party, I'd say that most of the guests are George's co-workers." George worked in the New York City offices of the State Department. "He invites a lot of people from his section and most of them usually bring along a friend. And I don't have to tell you how wild these foreign service types are."

Victoria nodded knowingly. "It's the international relations degree. It's affected us all, I fear."

"You're probably right. Here, try some of this pumpkin soup." Sue handed her a small bowl.

"Clever way of serving it, just hollowing out a huge pumpkin like that."

"Only the best for George. He decided to have the party catered this year. That's why we have all these lovely little signs telling us what these goodies are."

"They might have gone a little overboard on the pumpkin, though," Victoria decided. "Pumpkin cookies, muffins—"

"Hey, this looks good! Kahlua coconut custard."

When their plates were full, Sue and Victoria moved over to a semiquiet corner of the crowded room to eat their goodies.

"The next holiday is Thanksgiving," Sue said while nibbling on a muffin. "Are you going home to Vermont the way you usually do?"

Victoria, having just taken a spoonful of soup, nodded.

"I wasn't sure that you would, what with Kyle being here and all."

Sue's comment made Victoria realize that she should check with Kyle and see what his Thanksgiving plans were. She didn't want to think of him being alone for the holidays. She looked around the room for him and found that he was alone right now. He was way on the other side of the room, sitting on the corner love seat.

When she was through eating, she filled another plate and brought it over for him. "Here you are." She sat down next to him. "I brought you some food."

He shook his head.

"I know the pumpkin soup looks strange, but it tastes very good. No? Okay, I'll set it on the table in case you get hungry later. Well, what do you think of the party so far? It's even larger than last year."

He grunted.

"I don't know half the people here," she admitted. "How about you? Do you recognize many of them?"

He shook his head.

"I was talking to Sue a little while ago and she reminded me that Thanksgiving is coming up next. Do you have any plans?"

Again he shook his head.

"If you'd like, you could come home with me," she offered, somewhat tentatively. She knew her parents wouldn't mind. They liked Kyle.

"Great."

She frowned at him. "Your voice sounds hoarse. Are you okay?"

He nodded.

"Is the costume still too warm?"

It wasn't until he leaned forward and whispered a few lewd suggestions as to how she could cool him off that Victoria realized she wasn't speaking to Kyle. This was some other mummy!

"I'm sorry, I made a mistake," she muttered. "I thought you were someone else."

The mummy was not in any hurry to let her go. He came closer, pinning her against the couch with one of his outstretched bandage-wrapped arms. "No mistake," he slurred. "You foun' the right guy. I could use some good nursing."

"You move any closer to her and you're going to be nursing a broken arm," Kyle stated in a dangerous voice.

Victoria looked up to see Kyle, wearing regular street clothes, glaring at them. Even with the crutches he looked ready to do someone bodily harm.

The mummy hastily backed away and jumped to his feet.

"Beat it," Kyle growled.

The mummy made a hasty getaway.

"I thought it was you," she said by way of explanation.

Kyle lowered himself into the seat next to her. "Thanks a lot. The guy's four inches shorter and about fifty pounds heavier than I am, Tory."

"He was sitting down. I didn't notice that, all I noticed was that he was wearing a mummy costume. Just like you were the last time I saw you. Why didn't you tell me you were going to change?"

"The costume got too hot. Besides, I was starting to feel ridiculous in that getup."

He certainly didn't look ridiculous in the tan chinos and white shirt he was wearing now. In her opinion, he looked too damn good for her peace of mind. Annoyed with her observations, she allowed that irritation to surface in her voice. "You could have warned me. It would have saved me from that oversexed mummy's clutches."

"He clutched you?"

"No."

"Well, he obviously did or said something to upset you. What was it?" Kyle demanded. The glint in his eyes was downright threatening.

"Nothing, really." Victoria laid her hand on his arm. "Forget it, please, Kyle." She felt the tensed muscles in his forearm relax as he unclenched his fists. She also felt the warmth of his bare skin travel through her fingertips, straight to her heart.

"You sure he didn't hurt you?"

She nodded, unable to speak. He was looking at her so protectively that hope flared within her. Was he jealous? Was that why he'd reacted so violently? After catching a clear look at the mummy across the room, she decided Kyle couldn't possibly be jealous of a five-foot-eight, two-hundred-and-thirty-pound bandage roll. Besides, you had to feel attracted to someone to feel jealous. She should know. She was reasoning from personal experience here.

She'd noticed the looks Kyle was getting from the single women in the room. One, dressed like a female vampire, was blatantly flirting with him, eyeing him as if he were her next victim. Sure, Victoria could pretend, but who was she really kidding? This was jealousy she was feeling, enough of it to turn her brown eyes green.

Of course, she had no right to feel jealous. Kyle was her friend, not her lover. He was free to come and go as he pleased. But she couldn't help being relieved that he showed no sign of returning the vampire's interest.

"Where does George find all these people to dress up like this?" Kyle shook his head as a man dressed as a six-pack of beer awkwardly tried to make his way to the refreshment table.

Victoria, who'd been busy admiring Kyle's profile, didn't hear his question.

When she didn't answer him, Kyle turned to look at her.

Caught in the act of staring at him, she blushed, feeling like an idiot.

Seeing the rosiness staining her cheeks, he said, "Aren't you warm in that outfit? Here, take off the cloak."

"No, that's okay...." she protested.

But it was too late. Kyle had already removed the navy cloak from her shoulders. Now *his* face became flushed.

Victoria's breath caught in her throat as he looked at her with hungry eyes.

Kyle knew he was staring, but he couldn't help himself. He felt as if he'd had all the air knocked out of him. The nurse's uniform hugged her breasts like a second skin and gave new meaning to the word "formfitting." The nipped-in waist only accentuated the pert thrust of her breasts.

Feeling as if he'd been hit with lightning, Kyle quickly slid the cloak back over her shoulders. "Cover up," he growled. "That outfit's practically indecent!"

Perversely, Victoria shook the cloak off. "It is not. I'm completely covered."

"I can see that. It's the *way* you're covered...."

"What about the way I'm covered?" she countered sweetly.

"Isn't it a little...tight?" He ran his finger around the inside of his shirt collar.

"I thought it fit rather well, actually."

"I'm surprised you can even breathe in it." Kyle knew *he* was having trouble breathing. This was the second time tonight that she'd taken his breath away. She'd done it earlier when she'd been helping him get ready for the party. She'd been wrapping long, narrow strips of white material around his right leg from his cast up past his knee. The feel of her fingers on his leg, even through his slacks, had been too much for him. He'd called a halt to her assistance, curtly saying he could do the rest himself.

She hadn't seemed upset at all. She'd cheerfully stepped back and let him complete what wrapping he could. Then she'd pitched in to help him wrap his arms, which he hadn't had the foresight to realize he couldn't do on his own. Through it all, she'd been calm and collected. Unlike Kyle who'd been hot and bothered.

Apparently he was the only one feeling this way. The memory of the kiss they'd shared a week ago still worried him. He was even having trouble sleeping at night, and he couldn't blame it all on twinges from his healing ankle. More likely it was twinges from his guilty conscience.

He'd kissed Tory. And it hadn't just been a platonic kiss. Even worse, he'd liked it. So had she, he'd thought. Or had it only been part of the act she'd agreed to? Had she just been helping him out? He didn't know what she thought anymore. He could barely keep track of his own thoughts, they were so muddled most of the time.

Complications. He didn't need any more complications in his life. Who did?

Their life became even more complicated a few days later, when someone began pounding on their apartment door at seven in the morning.

Bam, bam, bam. Victoria reached out a hand to turn off her radio alarm clock before realizing that the noise wasn't the beat of some new song, it was someone pounding on the door. Pulling on her serviceable flannel robe, Victoria opened her bedroom door to go see what was going on. She met Kyle in the hallway.

"Who's making that racket?" she asked him.

"I don't know." He was disappointed to see that she wasn't wearing the black satin number. "Were you expecting anyone?"

"No. What about you?"

He shook his head. "You wait here. I'll go see who it is." He turned away from her and used the crutches to propel himself down the hallway to the front door.

"Who is it?" Kyle yelled.

"The painters."

"What painters?" Victoria asked.

When Kyle turned to answer her, he almost bumped her. She was standing right behind him. "I thought I told you to wait in the hallway!"

"You thought right. That's what you told me."

"Then what are you doing here by the front door?"

"I think you should be more concerned with what *painters* are doing at our front door."

She stepped around him and peeked through the peep hole. Sure enough, she saw three men dressed in white overalls and caps that read A-1 Painting. "They look like painters, all right," she said before Kyle tugged her away from the door.

"Would you just stay out of the way until I find out what's going on here?"

Kyle opened the door an inch, a threatening scowl marring his face. "What do you want?"

"We've got orders to paint this apartment today."

"Written orders? Let me see them."

Victoria saw a folded piece of paper shoved through the small crack between the open door and the frame.

Just as Kyle had suspected, the work order was signed A. Dinkman. "We weren't notified about any painters. You'll have to come back later."

"Can't do that. Your apartment is the last one left to be painted. We've got a signed work order to paint this one today. If you've got a problem with that, call the building manager."

"I intend to," Kyle muttered.

"Go ahead. We'll wait here."

"Well?" Victoria asked as Kyle shut the door in obvious irritation.

"Dinkman made arrangements to have the apartment painted without notifying us."

"He's not supposed to do that, is he?"

"No. I'm going to call him right now and remind him of that fact."

"Wait a minute. Are you sure he didn't notify you? I seem to remember there being a letter in that pile of mail that came while you were out of town."

"There was a letter from Dinkman in there?"

"I think there might have been. Didn't you find it when you went through the pile?"

"I haven't finished going through the pile yet."

"Kyle!"

"Well, you should have told me that there was a letter from Dinkman. I told you to open anything that looked important."

"And I told you that I hadn't had a chance to go through the mail that arrived the day before you did. I put it right at the top of the pile and you assured me that you'd take care of it." She impatiently shoved her hair out of her eyes. She couldn't cope with all this uproar, not without having completed her morning yoga first. "So now what do we do?"

Kyle shrugged. "It looks like we let the painters in."

Along with the painters came the smell of cigar smoke. "Please put that thing out," Victoria said to the man chewing on an inch-thick brown stub.

"Sure thing, lady." The man dropped the stub into his empty paint bucket.

Shuddering at his cavalier disposal of the vile-smelling object, Victoria gathered the lapels of her robe closer to her throat and retreated to the sanctuary of her room. She attempted a relaxing yoga session but was forced to quit because the noise of the painters kept distracting her. Gathering up her clothes, she hurried into the bathroom and locked the door.

A shower helped restore some of her usual orderly calm. She plaited her freshly washed hair into a neat French braid, one of her favorite styles. Her dress was also a favorite, a wraparound coat dress in a warm rust color. An autumn basic. She applied makeup in matching fall tones: olive shadow for her eyes, coral blush for her cheeks and russet lipstick. A pair of discreet gold hoop earrings and an oversize gold watch were the finishing touches.

The workmen were already setting up their ladders and drop cloths in the living room when she walked into the kitchen to get her grapefruit juice. The haphazardness of their operation did not increase her confidence in their abilities.

"How long will this job take?" she asked them.

"We'll have it done by tonight."

Just to be on the safe side, she confirmed that claim with another painter. "Listen, you guys are sure you'll be finished and out of here by this evening, right?"

"No problem, lady."

The sight of the ladder coming perilously close to Kyle's shelf of geodes distracted her from further questioning. She watched as the youngest of the trio of painters casually tugged one corner of a drop cloth over the shelving unit in what was clearly an afterthought. That did it. She edged closer and began gathering up a few of her favorite knickknacks.

"No need to move anything, ma'am" the painter said. "We'll handle it."

That was what she was afraid of. She could only imagine the way they'd handle her hand-blown glass lamp or her collection of David Winter cottages. She shuddered just thinking about it. She skipped breakfast in favor of collecting her favorite pieces and locking them in a closet.

Sensing her agitation, Kyle said, "Don't worry, I'll be here to keep an eye on these guys. You go on to work, I'll take care of things here."

"Are you sure?"

"Positive. Go, or you'll be late again."

Victoria left. But when she got home she found that the painters hadn't held up their end of the bargain. Oh, they were gone all right, just as they'd said they'd be. But they weren't finished painting. In fact, they'd stopped in the middle of her bedroom, having painted only three out of four walls. White drop cloths covered the furniture, and heavy-duty plastic covered the floor. Two ladders were propped against the unpainted wall.

She went looking for Kyle. He was in the den, obviously in the middle of a long-distance business call.

This room was untouched by the chaos that reigned in her room.

Seeing her, Kyle motioned for her to come in and sit down. He hung up a short while later. "You're home early."

"No, I'm not."

He shot a quick look at his watch. "I didn't realize it was this late."

"What happened with the painters?" she demanded.

"Now, don't get hysterical, they'll be back first thing in the morning to finish your room, the bathroom and this room. They ran out of time."

"What am I supposed to do until then? Where am I supposed to sleep tonight?"

"You can have my bed, and I'll sleep on the couch in the living room."

She ignored his offer. "I thought you were going to supervise the painters. What happened?"

"Nothing happened."

"That's what it looks like. It looks like nothing happened the way it was supposed to. They were supposed to be finished by tonight."

"A slight miscalculation on their part," he admitted. "They did get the kitchen, dining and living rooms and most of your room done."

"I can't believe this. The entire apartment is filled with paint fumes."

"That's why the windows are all open."

"Do you know what the temperature is supposed to be tonight? In the forties. We'll freeze if we keep the windows open."

"Studies say you sleep better when it's cool."

"Cool, not frozen," she retorted. "It's already freezing in here." She shivered and ran her hands up and down her arms in an effort to chase away the chill.

"You'd think that, growing up in Vermont the way you did, you'd be used to the cold," Kyle teased her.

Victoria was not amused. She'd always had a low tolerance for coldness. The only way she'd made it through those icy Vermont winters had been to bundle up when outside and turn up the thermostat when inside. But no matter how high the thermostat was turned, there was no way the apartment's radiators would be able to keep up when the windows were wide open.

Not that Kyle would notice. The fact that he was always warm, regardless of the temperature, was just an added annoyance in an already irritating situation. However, she was not about to discuss thermodynamics with him.

"I'm going to go make some tea," she announced with regal dignity.

She was already in the kitchen before Kyle remembered that he hadn't finished cleaning up the incriminating evidence left on the dining room table. Grabbing his crutches, he hauled himself upright and swung down the hallway, but he was already too late. She'd found the dealt-out deck of cards and the pot of winnings in the middle.

Suddenly it all fell into place. "You were playing poker with those painters, weren't you?" She shook her head in disbelief. "I left a real fox to guard the henhouse."

"The barnyard simile escapes me," he retorted.

"Instead of making sure those painters got the job done, you actually distracted them from their work."

"They were entitled to a lunch break, Tory."

"How long did the lunch break last, Kyle? Three hours? Four?"

"I resent your implication."

"Well, I resent being forced out of my room and having to sleep on the couch tonight."

"I told you I'd sleep on the damn couch."

"Right. I'm going to make an already injured man sleep on a couch that's at least five inches too short for him. Forget it."

"Sure, go ahead, play the martyr and try and make me feel guilty."

"You should feel guilty. This is all your fault."

"How do you figure that?"

"If you'd have opened your mail like you said you were going to, you would have known that the painters were coming this morning and we could have prepared accordingly. Failing that, you could at least have made sure they got the job done the way they were supposed to. You're a troubleshooter for a construction company. I thought I could leave you here to troubleshoot. When I left, you said you'd take care of things."

"The painters packed up while I was taking an important phone call from overseas. But I made sure that they'd be back first thing in the morning."

"Great, that helps a lot."

"Maybe if you stopped making mountains out of molehills you'd see that it's not such a big deal. What's done is done. There's no sense getting so upset about it."

"Fine, you can stay here and be calm and cold. I'm going someplace warm and welcoming."

"Wait a second. Where are you going?"

"Out to dinner. If I stay here any longer, the paint fumes are going to make me sick." She put her coat on again. But she couldn't leave without asking, "Do you want me to bring you back something to eat?"

Kyle shook his head. "I'll order something in."

"Fine."

Victoria ate a solitary dinner at a Greek restaurant on the corner of First and Forty-ninth Streets. The Athenian chicken there always made her feel better. Unfortunately, the apartment was still freezing when she got home. She started shivering as soon as she took off her coat. The smell of chicken chow mein was now mixed in with the paint fumes. Apparently Kyle had ordered Chinese.

He was in the den—or *his* room, as Victoria had come to think of it. He was watching the small color television in there instead of the larger set in the living room. He held up the white container he was eating out of as she walked by. "There's still some left. Want any?" She shook her head and walked on.

Getting what she needed out of her bedroom was like completing an obstacle course. It took her a while to dig out a long flannel nightgown, a thick robe and a pair of warm socks. Then she gathered up her pillow and her comforter. An electric blanket would have been nice, but hers was on the blink.

With her arms full, Victoria marched back down the hallway to the living room. After changing clothes in the bathroom, she made up the couch with some spare linens and arranged her comforter and her pillow into a comfortable configuration. Then she turned on the TV and watched the end of a movie.

By the time the local news came on at eleven, she'd decided that the flannel nightgown and robe would not be warm enough. So she headed back down the hall to her room and found a thick sweatshirt and a pair of sweatpants. She briefly considered taking a hot bath to warm up, but the idea of taking off her clothes in such frigid air dissuaded her. Instead, she locked herself in the bathroom and prepared to change from the nightgown into the sweatshirt and pants. But after further consideration she decided not to abandon the warmth of the nightgown after all. It seemed better to just add the sweatshirt and pants, both of which retained the chill from her room. The layered look was in, right?

Victoria had finished brushing her teeth and was heading back to the living room when she met Kyle in the hallway.

Looking at her outfit, he grinned. "Not cold, are you?"

"No, I always dress for bed this way," she retorted.

"You look like Nanook of the North."

She glared at him. Did he have to stand there radiating heat like that? His pajama top wasn't even buttoned.

"Have you calmed down yet?"

"No."

"Still insisting on sleeping on the couch?"

"Yes."

"Still mad at me?"

"Yes." His comment about her bundled-up look had refueled her anger. Besides, being angry made her feel a little warmer. Not much, but a little.

"You're being incredibly stubborn, do you know that?"

"Thank you for that valuable piece of information, Kyle. If you're done lecturing me, I'd like to get some sleep."

"Fine." Now he sounded irritated, too. "Go right ahead."

"Fine. I will."

"Good night."
"Good night."
She marched past him with her head held high.
But sleep was not easy to come by.
In his room, Kyle punched his pillow and muttered, "Women!" while out in the living room, Victoria yanked the covers up to her ears and muttered, "Men!"
It was not a restful night for either of them.

Six

Victoria was up before sunrise the next morning. What little sleep she had gotten had been fraught with vivid dreams inspired by the cold. Several times she'd woken up shivering with images of icebergs still fresh in her mind. Closing her eyes determinedly, she'd made it through the night by promising herself a deliciously warm, sinfully caloric breakfast in the morning.

So here she was, rewarding herself with a huge slice of homemade almond coffee cake from the same Greek restaurant she'd gone to last night. They did their own baking on the premises, and the coffee cake was still warm from the oven.

The chill was finally leaving her body, thanks in part to the hot shower she'd taken earlier and the skirt and sweater set she was wearing. Aside from being warm, the red silk-and-angora-blend outfit was very flattering. She dared anyone to compare her to Nanook of the North this morning!

In fact, she was the recipient of a number of appreciative looks from the Greek waiters. Their dark-eyed attention was a much-needed morale booster. It was nice to be noticed, to be appreciated. The only problem was that she wanted only one man looking at her that way—Kyle.

He'd still been sound asleep when she'd peeked in on him before leaving the apartment. She'd resented the fact that he was contentedly snoozing without any sign of the discomfort she'd suffered all night long. He at least could have tucked the covers up to his ears. But no, with the blankets and sheets twisted down around his waist, he'd lain sprawled out on the bed—looking magnificently male.

Normally she wasn't the kind of person to hold a grudge, but she was still mad at him. Unfortunately, she was afraid she was in grave danger of becoming mad *about* him as well. Because as much as she liked to tell herself otherwise, she *hadn't* forgotten the kiss they'd shared in the back of the carriage ten days ago. The memory had stubbornly refused to go away, even though she'd brushed it under a mental rug.

Obviously she was the only one who was having trouble forgetting. It was clear to her that Kyle saw her no differently. He continued to treat her as his buddy and nothing more. With 20/20 hindsight Victoria realized that pretending to be Kyle's girlfriend might not have been such a bright idea after all. Instead of affirming that she preferred his friendship to anything else, the masquerade had her wishing for more. But her feelings weren't returned—that much was plain to see. She'd have to continue playing the part of pal and nothing more. She

TEAR OFF HERE AND MAIL THIS CARD TODAY!

MAIL THIS FREE-GIFT COMPUTER CARD

SILHOUETTE FREE GIFT DEPT.

to receive 4 FREE Silhouette Desires®... *PLUS* **a FREE Surprise Bonus!**

Use this heart to get a FREE SURPRISE BONUS!

FREE!
AFFIX THIS STICKER IN SPACE AT RIGHT

Yes! Send me 4 Free Silhouette Desires plus A Free Surprise Bonus. Then send me six new Silhouette Desires each month and bill me just $2.24 per book (26¢ less than retail). No postage and handling charges. If I am not fully satisfied, I may return a shipment and cancel at any time. The 4 Free Books and Surprise Bonus remain mine to keep.

225 CIL JAYM

☐ MR.
☐ MRS.
☐ MISS

FIRST NAME _____ INITIAL _____ LAST NAME

PRINT YOUR NAME HERE FOR DATA PROCESSING (Please PRINT in ink)

ADDRESS _____ APT. _____

CITY _____ STATE _____ ZIP _____

Offer limited to one per household and not valid for present Desire subscribers. Prices subject to change.

FREE GIFT DEADLINE: | S | E | P | T | 3 | 0 | 1 | 9 | 8 | 8 |

PLACE GOLD HEART HERE
to receive your FREE Surprise Bonus

```
DATA PROCESSING *1348
00000000000000000000
45 46 47 48 49 50 51 52 53 54 55 56
1 1 1 1 1 1 1 1 1 1 1 1
2222222222222222222222
```

TEAR OFF HERE AND MAIL THIS CARD TODAY!

Printed in U.S.A.

APPROVED OFFER
FREE-GIFT OFFER

BUSINESS REPLY CARD
FIRST CLASS   PERMIT NO. 717   BUFFALO, NY

POSTAGE WILL BE PAID BY ADDRESSEE

Silhouette Books®

901 Fuhrmann Blvd.,
P.O. Box 1867
Buffalo, NY 14240-9952

NO POSTAGE
NECESSARY
IF MAILED
IN THE
UNITED STATES

couldn't embarrass Kyle by letting him see that she'd "gone and gotten sentimental on him"—and over him.

Later that morning Kyle called her at work, something he normally didn't do. "You left before I woke up this morning. Does that mean you're still mad at me?"

Aware of Mr. Molenaar's eagle eye, she kept her reply brief. "It might."

"How about if I told you that the painters are done with your bedroom? They're almost done with the bathroom, and then there's just my room left. They'll be out of here by lunch time, and everything will be back to normal, you'll see."

If only it were that simple, she thought to herself. But she had the feeling it would be some time before her turbulent emotions were "back to normal."

"Tory? Did you hear what I said?"

"Yes, I heard. That's good news."

"So you're not mad at me anymore?"

"No."

"Good." He sounded satisfied. "I'll see you when you get home."

When she did get home, the smell of paint fumes no longer filled the apartment. Instead, there was a delicious smell of...roses!

She looked around the living room, expecting to see a huge bouquet somewhere. All she saw was Kyle standing in the hallway with a sheepish expression on his face.

"I guess I went a little overboard on the air freshener," he finally said.

Victoria felt foolishly disappointed. *What did you expect?* she angrily asked herself. *That Kyle had ordered roses for you? Be realistic.*

"At least it smells better than the paint fumes," she said with forced cheerfulness. She slid out of her coat and hung it in the closet. Only then did she notice the large paper-wrapped item sitting on the floor next to her umbrella stand. "What's this?"

He shrugged. "Open it up and find out."

She picked up the package, which was wrapped in florist's paper, and carried it to the coffee table. She looked at Kyle for a clue, but he was wearing his poker face. Her heart quickened with excitement as she ripped away the paper, revealing a beautiful floral display with white mums and exotic orange birds of paradise.

"Kyle, it's lovely," she breathed.

"Who are they from?" he asked her.

She blinked in surprise. "They're not from you?"

He shook his head.

"Oh." Victoria swallowed the sudden lump in her throat.

"Isn't there a card?"

Her trembling fingers latched on to the small white envelope, grateful for the distraction. Then she noticed the name on the envelope. "Wait a minute! These aren't for me, they're for you!" She dropped the envelope as if it had bitten her.

Kyle swore softly. There was only one person who would send him flowers. He knew it, and so did Tory. He grabbed her arm as she walked past him. "Wait. There's no reason to let a perfectly good floral arrangement go to waste, is there? Pretend I sent it to you."

More pretending? She'd already had her fill. She slowly pulled away. "You'd better open the card."

"Forget the damn card."

She wouldn't look at him. "I've got to change." She slipped past him, went to her room and quietly closed the door.

When Victoria returned to the living room she found Kyle sitting in his recliner with another lapful of blueprints. There was no sign of the floral arrangement.

"I tossed it out," he said. Feeling uncomfortable about how to proceed from there, Kyle tried to make amends—even though he didn't know what he was making amends for. "If I'd have known you wanted flowers, I would have ordered some for you."

"Don't be ridiculous. Why should you send me flowers?"

"Because you've been such a good sport about everything."

"That's what friends are for," she replied flatly.

"Are you all right? You sound funny."

"I'm tired. I didn't get much sleep last night."

"I'm sorry about that." He seemed genuinely remorseful. "Let me make it up to you. How about brunch this Sunday? What's that place on top of the World Trade Center called—Windows to the World? You've always wanted to go there, haven't you? Here's your chance."

"It's Windows *on* the World. And is this supposed to be another date to convince Angelica that you're already taken?" she demanded bluntly.

"No. It's just you and me going out together and having brunch."

Sounds like a date to me, she thought to herself. But Kyle probably considered it the same as going out with Jeff or George. Victoria felt depressed. "We'll go Dutch," she stated. A girl had to have some pride.

Her statement irritated Kyle for some reason. "I invited you, I'll pay for it. What's the big deal?"

"You don't have to try and buy my forgiveness," she shot back.

"Are we having another fight here?"

Her anger disappeared as quickly as it had flared. "No."

"I'm glad. Truce?"

"Truce."

"Then it's all settled. I'll pay for brunch, and we'll have it at Windows on the World."

Sunday morning Victoria looked in the mirror and shook her head. Here she was, getting dressed to go out again with Kyle. This time she was going into it with her eyes open, she told herself. This time it was just a friendly brunch, not an exercise in romance. Brilliant sunshine instead of the romantic shadows of evening. No problem. It was like falling off a horse, you simply had to get up and ride again, proving to yourself that you were not spooked.

To do that she wore a red wool jersey dress with a flared skirt that swirled around her legs as she walked. It made her feel good. She was still feeling good when she and Kyle entered the oversize elevator on the ground floor of the World Trade Center.

Balancing himself on his crutches, Kyle headed straight for the elevator's back wall. Turning around was a little tricky, but he managed it. Facing forward now, he leaned back against the wall. There was a reason for his maneuvering. He'd ridden this elevator before and knew about its rocketlike takeoff. Victoria was not similarly prepared. One minute she was standing upright, the next she was plastered against Kyle's chest.

"I'm sorry," she gasped. "I lost my balance." She hastily stepped away, fearful that she'd hurt his injured ankle by bumping into him that way. "Are you okay?"

Kyle was looking at her with a strange expression on his face.

When he didn't answer her question right away, she became concerned. "Did I hurt you?"

"No." He shook his head as if to clear it of disconcerting images. "I'm fine."

It was a welcome diversion when the elevator arrived at the top. Maneuvering on his crutches took all his attention, thereby preventing him from dwelling on the surge of emotion he'd felt when Victoria's body had been pressed so tightly against his own. It wasn't until they were shown to a windowside table that Kyle allowed himself to think about what had happened.

He stared at Victoria as the maître d' held out the chair for her. Things had been much less complicated when he'd only seen her as a friend, not as a woman—a very attractive woman. He glared at a man at the next table who was staring at Victoria and then felt foolish for doing so. What was going on here?

He opened the menu and brooded behind it. He found it very disconcerting to have these feelings for Tory. When she'd stumbled against him like that, he'd been hit by a surge of attraction that still had him confused. What was more, he could have sworn that he'd seen a matching awareness in her startled brown eyes when she'd looked up at him.

Pretending an interest in the view, he watched Tory out of the corner of his eye. She seemed perfectly calm now. At ease. Comfortable.

He forced himself to relax and concentrated on his surroundings instead of his feelings. "Nice view, hmm?" he noted in a deliberately offhand sort of voice.

Victoria nodded. "I've lived in this city...what...nine years now, and I'm still impressed by a panorama like this."

"There's an excitement about New York, especially its skyline, that you don't find anyplace else," Kyle agreed.

The excitement Victoria was feeling had nothing to do with the city—and everything to do with Kyle. Just being with him had always made her feel warm and happy inside. They'd always been able to talk easily. They'd never been at a loss for words before.

But sometimes lately she'd find herself suddenly becoming tongue-tied. Or she'd unexpectedly lose track of what they were talking about because she was listening to the way his words sounded rather than to the actual words themselves. She'd watch his mouth and wonder what it would be like to have him kiss her again. She'd watch his eyes and wonder what it would be like to see them darken with desire for her. Did Kyle ever wonder the same kind of things about her, or was she really the only one suffering from this affliction? She sighed and returned her thoughts to the menu in front of her.

After Kyle had placed their orders—an omelet for himself and pancakes with apples and raisins for Victoria—they both relaxed, enjoying the view and each other's company. But there was a certain spark that hadn't been between them before, a certain sexual charge. Oh, it was understated, but they were both aware of it.

Their hands touched as they reached for a roll at the same time. Their eyes met. *Did you feel it, too?* they seemed to be asking each other. Victoria searched for an answer in Kyle's eyes, just as he searched for an answer in hers. Was the answer yes or no? Neither one could be sure.

A touch, a look, and my heart races, Victoria thought to herself. There was something going on between them here, she could feel it. Could he? The looks he was giving her offered her some hope that she wasn't the only one feeling this way.

It didn't take her long to realize that all the speculation was distracting her from enjoying the magic of the moment. Instead of questioning it all, she simply sat back and relaxed. So did Kyle, and they ended up having such a good time that they forgot to wonder about all the "how comes" and the "what ifs."

The time went quickly. The pleasure they got from each other's company outshone everything else, even the fine food. After the meal Kyle ordered an additional pot of tea for Victoria and a third cup of coffee for himself, more as an excuse to linger than anything else.

Victoria was in no hurry to leave, either. She dreamily stared out the window, pleased with the world and everything in it. "The Statue of Liberty looks so small from here, doesn't it?"

Kyle nodded. "Have you been out there since they renovated it?"

"Actually, I've never gone to see the statue at all," she admitted. "Another one of the many things I've been meaning to do. Somehow, when you live here, you don't have the time to see the sights."

"We've got time today. We could take the ferry across."

She looked at him in surprise. "You're kidding."

"Moi?" He raised his eyebrows and pointed a finger at his chest. "I never kid."

"And if I believe that, I'll bet you'd like to sell me one of those bridges over there...."

He grinned and told her, "That one's already sold. Bought by a nice little old lady just last week. So what do you say, are you up for a visit over to Liberty Island or not?"

"You're serious?"

"Absolutely."

"But what about your ankle?"

"What about it?"

"It's broken."

"I had noticed that, Tory."

"Don't you think that—"

"I think you worry too much. Are you interested, yes or no?"

She was interested, all right. "Yes."

"Good."

Victoria felt better than good, she felt on top of the world. But after a trip to the ladies' room a few minutes later, her good spirits tumbled back to earth. Victoria was leaning closer to the oversize mirror, applying a new coat of lipstick, when she heard a familiar feminine voice drawl, "Fancy meeting you here."

It was Angelica. The unexpectedness of her appearance startled Victoria so much that she almost smeared her lipstick clear across her cheek. She capped the tube before she could do further damage. "Mrs. Van Horne," she murmured calmly. "What a surprise."

"Are you here with Kyle?"

"Of course. Are you here with your husband?"

"Naturally."

Personally, Victoria didn't see anything natural about the situation between Angelica and her husband, but she kept her opinion to herself.

The silence dragged as Angelica looked her over from head to toe. "You're not Kyle's type at all," Angelica finally stated. "He likes brunettes."

Victoria refused to be intimidated. "He may like brunettes, but he loves me." His love might be platonic instead of romantic, but it was a type of love nonetheless.

Victoria's conviction threw Angelica. "You say that as if you believe it. I suppose you love him, too?"

"Yes, I do." Only she probably loved him in more ways than he loved her, she admitted to herself.

Angelica gave her a narrow-eyed stare. "I do believe you're telling the truth. You really do love Kyle. But that doesn't necessarily mean the feeling is returned, now does it? We'll just have to see what happens, won't we?"

"What's that supposed to mean?"

"It means that this isn't over. I'm not giving up just yet. May the best woman win."

"Wait a minute! You make it sound as if this were all some sort of game. It's not. People's feelings are involved here. You can't treat them as if they were pawns."

"Why not?" There was bitterness beneath the carelessness as Angelica added, "That's how my husband treats me."

"Then that's something you should take up with your husband," Victoria quietly suggested. "Anything else is pretty pointless in the long run."

Angelica's eyes widened, and for a moment Victoria thought she might have gotten through to her. It was wishful thinking, because Angelica said, "I'll tell you what's pointless—this little charade of yours. As I said before, may the best woman win." A moment later she was gone, leaving behind the smell of expensive perfume and the memory of a catty smile.

Victoria took an extra few moments to compose herself. She had several disturbing thoughts to contend with. The major one was, what if Kyle had planned this morning's outing as another display for Angelica's benefit? He'd told her that his reasons for inviting her had nothing to do with Angelica, but it was a bit too coincidental that Angelica should show up in the same place and at the same time they did in a city as large as New York.

Had Kyle lied to her? She didn't want to believe that. Tempting though it was, she knew she couldn't hide out in the ladies' room any longer. Kyle was waiting for her. And he was the only one who had the answers to the questions she was asking herself.

Kyle was sitting on an upholstered bench in the foyer, his crutches resting beside him. The moment she joined him he tugged her down onto the bench beside him. "Okay, you want to tell me what happened in there?"

"I beg your pardon?"

"I meant with Angelica. I saw her come out a few minutes before you did."

"Did you know she'd be here?"

He looked her straight in the eye and said, "No."

She believed him. Too bad Angelica didn't believe her. She sighed, realizing that Kyle would have to be told of this latest development. "She doesn't believe that you and I are romantically involved," Victoria said in a quiet undertone. "She said I wasn't your type. Apparently your preference for brunettes is well-known."

"I'd choose you over a brunette any day."

"Sure."

"I mean it. I didn't ask a brunette to brunch, I asked you. I didn't invite a brunette to go see the statue, I asked you."

"Because I'm your pal."

"Because you're the one I wanted to be with."

Her brown eyes met his blue ones. Caught up in the possibilities she saw there, she couldn't look away. Neither could he.

"You're the one I want to be with," he repeated softly, almost to himself.

For one heartbeat everyone else in the busy foyer faded away, leaving only the two of them. Then, unsettled by the powerful force of the visual bond between them, Kyle turned away.

When he spoke again, his voice was deliberately light. "If that's just another way of saying we're pals, then so be it. Do we have to analyze everything?"

Victoria, too breathless from what had just transpired to speak, shook her head.

"Then let's just forget all this, go out and get some fresh air and pay a visit to Lady Liberty."

The air was indeed fresh and a little on the cool side, Victoria observed as the ferry headed out from Battery Park toward Liberty Island. But when she considered that it was early November already she realized that the weather was actually quite temperate. She and Kyle were seated on a wooden bench near the entryway on the ferry's lower deck, so Kyle wouldn't have far to walk.

As the boat bounced over the choppy waters of New York Harbor, Victoria was frequently jostled against Kyle's side. He put his arm around her and tugged her close. She savored the moment. It wasn't a time for thought, it was a time for pleasure—simple pleasure, like sharing a smile over the excited antics of a little Korean girl a few feet away.

She and Kyle didn't talk much during the short ride. There wasn't any need, and there wasn't much opportunity. The noise level was quite loud, as hundreds of voices speaking various languages all mixed together in the unique babble that Victoria had always associated with New York City.

Once they reached the island they separated themselves from the crowd and walked to one of the nearby park benches. This section of the park was almost deserted as most people rushed to enter the base of the statue. Here it was quiet. A few leaves still stubbornly clung to the dark skeletons of the trees. They rustled in the breeze, as did the American flag, proudly waving from the top of a flagpole.

"That's where we were," Victoria said as she picked out the World Trade Center from the distinctive Manhattan skyline laid out before them.

They had a front-row seat. To their left was Ellis Island, and to their right was the statue itself. From this angle the subtle details were more noticeable—the intricate draping on the back of Lady Liberty's robes, the graceful strength of her right arm as it held up the torch.

"You should really go inside and see the display they've got in the Museum of Immigration," Kyle told her. "And you should take the elevator up to the top of the pedestal. You get a great view of the statue from the balcony there."

"I like the view from here just fine," she said.

They were quiet for a few moments, comfortable with their thoughts.

"You know, my grandparents entered this country through Ellis Island," Kyle murmured.

"Really? I didn't know that."

Kyle nodded. "They came over right after World War I. In fact, they met while being processed at Ellis. It turned out they were from the same county back in Ireland, county Wicklow, from towns that were only ten miles apart. Yet they'd never met until they reached Ellis."

"It must have been fate."

"Must have been. My grandfather was the youngest of six brothers. The oldest had come to the States several years earlier and was doing well enough in the construction trade to bring the rest of the family over to work for him."

"What about your grandmother?"

"She was coming to work in her cousin's tavern as a barmaid. The way my grandfather told the story, he waited almost a year before looking her up because he wanted to be established before going to court her. When he had enough money put away, he went after her. My grandmother's version is slightly different, however. She claims that he'd forgotten all about her, while she'd had a crush on him ever since they'd met. So she'd made it a point to have one of her many cousins look him up and bring him 'round to the bar. Whatever happened, it worked out. Last year they celebrated their fifty-fifth wedding anniversary."

"What a wonderful story, Kyle. And so romantic." *They don't make marriages like that anymore,* she thought to herself. *Built to last. Solid.* And she particularly liked the part about Kyle's grandmother harboring a crush on his grandfather. She could definitely relate to that. "My grandparents came here through Ellis, too. My mother's parents immigrated from Alsace-Lorraine right before the First World War."

"I heard somewhere that nearly one out of every two American families can trace their roots back to someone who went through Ellis Island."

"A lot of dreams must have started there," she said softly.

"A lot of those dreams didn't come true."

"A lot did."

"You're an optimist."

"You're a pessimist."

"That's right," he agreed, "and proud of it."

They both smiled at the familiar exchange, which dated back to their college days.

"What about your dreams, Kyle? And don't tell me you don't have any, because I know that's not true. Where do you see yourself ten years from now?"

"Not out here freezing my tail off, that's for sure."

She playfully socked him in the arm. "I'm serious."

"So am I. It's cold out here."

"This from the human furnace?" she asked mockingly. "The man who feels no chill?"

"Feel my hand." He held one out to her.

She took it. "You feel warm to me."

"That's because your hands are like icicles. Here, give them to me." He held her fingers up to his mouth and blew warm air on them. "There, is that better?"

Victoria nodded. Touching him, being touched by him, felt so right, so natural. Did he feel the same way, too? Was he seeing her as Tory, his pal, or Victoria, the woman? Nervous excitement shot through her, and her hand began to tremble. She quickly snatched it away from him.

Kyle looked at her in surprise.

"That tickled," she explained lamely as she tucked her hand in her coat pocket, safely out of temptation's way. "So go on and tell me, where do you see yourself ten years from now?"

"I don't know. Owning my own consulting business, if I'm lucky. What about you? Where do you see yourself?"

"Hopefully, by then I'll have completed my master's degree and I'll have moved up the professional ladder, either at the UN or elsewhere. Maybe I'll be married, hopefully have some kids. Two would be nice. A girl and a boy. I'll live outside of the city, Connecticut if we could afford it."

"We?"

"My future husband, whoever he may be, and I."

"What kind of guy is he going to be, this future husband of yours?"

"He'll be warm and understanding, have a great sense of humor, be able to laugh at himself—" She stopped, suddenly aware that she was actually describing Kyle. Could he tell?

Apparently not, she realized when he said, "The guy sounds like some kind of paragon. Have you met him yet?"

"I'm not sure. Hey, how come you're the one asking all the questions and I'm the one who's giving all the answers?"

"Just clever maneuvering on my part," he stated modestly.

"Do you see yourself as being married ten years from now?"

Kyle nodded slowly. "The two kids sound nice, too. A boy and a girl."

"And what will your future wife be like? Brunette, blonde?" *Go ahead and fish, why don't you, Victoria?* she chastised herself. She just hadn't been able to resist the temptation of asking.

He gave her question some thought before answering. "I'm not sure what she'll *look* like, but I am sure what she'll *be* like. She'll be—" Kyle paused as he realized what he'd been about to say. He'd been about to say, *She'll be like you, Tory.* And that discovery scared the hell out of him.

Seven

Victoria's mind was not on her work the next morning. The rainy Monday had most people wishing they could have stayed home. But Victoria's reasons for being distracted went beyond the weather or a case of the Monday-morning blues. She couldn't concentrate because of Kyle. *He'd* done this to her.

Of course it hadn't been intentional on his part, but their friendly jaunt over to see the Statue of Liberty had, for her at least, turned into an intimate sharing of hopes and dreams. Once again something that had started out simple had ended up getting complicated.

She'd thought everything was going fine yesterday when Kyle had suddenly just clammed up. He'd hardly spoken two words during the ferry ride back, and even when they'd gotten to the apartment he'd remained quiet and preoccupied. At first she'd worried that his ankle was giving him pain, but he'd quickly and somewhat curtly disabused her of that notion. Then he'd retreated to his room, saying he had work to do.

So did she, as the pile of paperwork on her desk this Monday morning confirmed. Bureaucratic red tape stopped for no man or woman. Sighing—something she'd been doing a lot of lately—she once again applied her attention to the documents in front of her. She'd finally gotten somewhat immersed in figuring out a tangled application form when Mr. Molenaar materialized beside her desk.

"I'd like to speak to you in my office," he said.

She closed the file she was working on and wondered what she could possibly have done to make her boss look so disapproving.

She soon found out.

"I've heard disturbing news, Victoria."

"What is it? What's happened?" He looked so stern that she was really concerned now.

"It's come to my attention that you are living with a man who is not your husband. Is this true?"

Victoria was flabbergasted. Here she was expecting some terrible diplomatic faux pas, and he was talking about her private life.

"Is this true?" he repeated.

Caught off guard, she nodded.

"I see. I'm disappointed in you, Victoria. I thought you understood what I was trying to do here in the protocol department. I thought you understood the responsibilities we have. We've got to set an example, to be above reproach in both our professional and our private lives. This kind of behavior is simply inappropriate."

"My private life has no bearing on how well I do my work," she protested.

"I disagree. When you're trying to project an image of dignity and formality, your private life is part of that image. I shouldn't have to tell you that, Victoria. After all, you've been here long enough to know how important decorum is. And you know how tight-knit the diplomatic community is."

"I hardly think the diplomatic community is going to concern itself with my private life. They've all got more important things to talk about."

"It's no use trying to minimize your mistake."

"I'm not trying to minimize anything," she stated. "I haven't done anything wrong."

"That is your opinion. I thought I'd made my views on the matter of diplomatic decorum clear when I became your supervisor."

She remembered the vague speech about higher standards and ideals he'd given her at that time.

"I may not have been able to have my views adopted as official policy in this department," he went on to say, "but it's my own personal policy, and it's not one I intend to reverse."

"I've got an official policy of my own, Mr. Molenaar, and that is that the details of my private life remain private," Victoria said firmly.

"Unless it interferes with your position here, which it is doing. I won't tolerate idle gossip about one of my employees, Victoria."

She already knew how widespread the grapevine was, how it exaggerated things completely out of proportion. That was why she'd always made it a point not to discuss anything personal at work. "Who's been gossiping? I don't discuss my private life with anyone here."

"And rightly so, but this was bound to come out sooner or later."

"You make it sound as if I've committed some terrible crime."

"Not a crime, but a definite violation of my policy." He went on at some length, lecturing her on the importance of setting a good example. He ended by advising her, "You'd do well to think about what I've said."

"I won't forget what you've told me," she returned. Her jaw actually hurt from the way she'd been gritting her teeth while he'd delivered his sermon.

It was only when she'd returned to her desk that she realized two things—the first was that she was shaking, and the second was that she hadn't thought to ask how Mr. Molenaar had found out about Kyle.

Instinct provided her with the answer to that question. Just yesterday Angelica had warned her, "It's not over yet." She didn't know how she knew, but she did know—somehow Angelica Van Horne was at the bottom of this. Somehow Angelica must have found out where she worked and decided to stir up trouble, something Angelica was very good at doing.

But how did Madame Man-eater find out where I work? Victoria asked herself. She'd only met the woman on two occasions. Mentally replaying both those meetings, she realized that she'd told Angelica herself that she worked at the UN—when the other woman had so condescendingly asked her if she worked in a bar. Victoria groaned. All it would have taken was one phone call to the switchboard for Angelica to locate her in the protocol department. A little additional research would have turned up the information that Victoria's boss was a very straitlaced individual with definite ideas about personal standards of behavior.

Victoria had no way of proving it, of course. There were probably others who could have notified her boss, or he could have found out by accident, but her gut reaction was that it had been Angelica. The woman seemed to have a talent for creating problems in the workplace—first at Kyle's workplace and now at hers.

The office atmosphere was naturally strained that afternoon as a result of her run-in with her boss. Although Mr. Molenaar made no further reference to the matter, his disapproval was evident in the way he spoke to her and looked at her.

By the time Victoria got home she was a bundle of nerves. *Definitely another hot-bath day,* she decided as she let herself into the apartment and headed straight for the bathroom without so much as a hello to Kyle. *I may stay in there until Thursday.*

The bath didn't help as much as it should have. She was still feeling wrung out afterward, so she made herself a cup of hot tea, another one of her surefire remedies for whatever ailed her. As often happened when she was really upset, Victoria focused her attention on the little picture rather than the larger chaos. The bigger the problem, the more microscopic were her concerns. It said something about her state of mind that she made sure the cup was sitting on the saucer just so, with the handle at precisely three o'clock and the string of the tea bag at six o'clock. She set the teaspoon next to the cup and saucer, arranging it so that it was perfectly straight, and then ruined the pristine effect by splashing hot water over the edge of the cup when she poured it from the kettle.

Swearing in French, she slammed the kettle back onto the stove and jammed her burned fingers into her mouth. While gathering a cloth to wipe up the water, she knocked over the tea canister, which fell into the sink with a clatter. She swore even louder this time.

"What's wrong?" Kyle yelled from the living room. He recognized trouble when he heard it.

"Nothing!" she yelled back, so frustrated she could have cried. "Not a damn thing!"

"O-kay," he said with the cautious disbelief of someone who knew her well. A few moments later he joined her in the kitchen. "You want to tell me about it?" he asked, propping himself on his crutches and reaching into the cookie jar.

"I spilled some water, that's all."

"Hmmm," he mumbled as he munched on a peanut butter cookie.

"What's that supposed to mean?" she demanded defensively.

"Calm down. What's the matter? Rough day at work?" He frowned when she laughed somewhat hysterically. "What do you say we retire to the couch in the other room and discuss this calmly and rationally?"

"There's nothing to discuss."

"Humor me. Come into the living room and sit down."

She followed him reluctantly.

"Okay, now tell me what happened," Kyle asked when they were seated next to each other.

"I told you."

"I mean what happened at work."

"I'd rather not talk about it, okay?"

"No, it's not okay. Something's bothering you, and I want to know what it is."

"I don't want to talk about it."

"Funny, you always used to talk about your problems with me."

"That was before."

"Before what?"

"Before my boss accused me of having loose moral standards!" she burst out angrily. "There, I said it, are you happy now?"

"Tory, you have higher standards than anyone I know, and anyone who tells you otherwise is an idiot. Suppose you start at the beginning and tell me exactly what happened."

She gave him a condensed version.

"Do you think that it would help if I called your boss and explained that we're just friends, that I don't normally live here with you, that I'm here now only because of my broken ankle?"

She shook her head.

"You don't think it would help?"

"He's got no right even asking."

"How did he find out we're living together?"

"I don't know." Suspecting Angelica was one thing, but telling Kyle about her suspicion without any proof to back it up was something else again.

"Hey." He reached out to touch her cheek with his hand. "I'm sorry you had such a rough time of it today." He rested his hand on her shoulder. A gentle tug, and she was in his arms. "It'll be okay," he whispered, running his hands down her back in a soothing display of reassurance.

His concern made her cry.

"Am I doing something wrong here or what?" he asked in feigned bewilderment.

She shook her head and burrowed closer.

Victoria couldn't have said exactly when the comforting changed into something else—something neither one of them could resist. It happened gradually, inexorably. But something was happening, and they both recognized it.

Lifting her face from his shoulder, she gazed at Kyle in confused anticipation. He was looking down at her as if seeing her for the first time. Oh so gently he wiped her tears away with his fingers. "Shh, it'll be all right," he whispered again, kissing her cheek as he spoke. One kiss turned into half a dozen, strewn from her temple to her chin.

Victoria's hands slid from his chest up to his shoulders and around his neck. She fingered the silky thickness of his hair where it touched the back of his collar. Touching him like that had a wonderfully liberating effect on her. Freed from her enforced inhibitions, she explored him like a detective searching for clues. Every detail—the nick on his chin where he'd cut himself shaving this morning, the curve of his ear, the strong line of his jaw—everything fascinated her. This was Kyle, but a Kyle she'd never seen before—a Kyle who was exploring her face with the same newfound sense of wonder with which she was exploring his.

It was only a matter of seconds before their lips met, parted and then met again. The kiss began as a gentle quest. He took only what she offered. She wanted only what he gave. But the more she offered, the more he gave, the more they both wanted. Caution was swept away as their real feelings took control.

The kiss deepened, progressing from tantalizing tenderness to powerful passion and exploring all the stages in between. His tongue began slowly wooing her parted lips with a sensual thoroughness that she'd always known he must possess. She'd dreamed of having him kiss her like this. But the reality was even better than anything her imagination had ever conjured up.

He made her want in a way she'd never wanted before. He made her feel eager to give him what she'd never given before—her heart, her love. As they drifted down onto the couch, all she could think of was how right this felt. To finally be in his arms was heaven. His body was a welcome weight resting on top of hers. He was wonderfully heavy, but not overwhelmingly so. Moaning softly, she wrapped her arms around his waist. But even as she was marveling at how perfectly they fit together, Kyle was moving away from her.

She felt the loss immediately. She opened eyes that were dazed with passion and saw him looking at her with a regretful expression on his face. The rejection she felt was immediate and incredibly painful.

Scrambling off the couch, she stood and faced him with proud defiance. "Nothing happened. Absolutely nothing. We both got a little carried away. No big deal. Forget about it."

"Easier said than done, Tory," he whispered as she marched down the hallway to her bedroom. He winced when he heard her door slam. "Well, this is a fine mess you've gotten yourself into, O'Reilly," he muttered to himself. "Now what are you going to do about it?"

Victoria was wondering the same thing herself. What was she going to do about Kyle? This latest incident was going to be much harder to forget than their first kiss had been. Make that downright impossible to forget, she mentally amended.

Since neither of them could go to the other for advice, they chose the next-best thing. They consulted another member of the gang. Victoria had a heart-to-heart with Sue at her place in Brooklyn, and Kyle invited Jeff over to the apartment for beer and conversation.

"You'd think I'd know better," Victoria groaned. "After seeing what Liz went through with Jeff, you'd think I'd have learned from that. But no. Here I am with a tangled mess on my hands. I'm attracted to Kyle. And Kyle, well, who knows what he thinks or feels."

"That might be your first priority," Sue suggested. "Finding out what Kyle thinks about this, how he feels about you."

"I'm afraid to find out."

"Why?"

Victoria shook her head. "I don't know. I feel so mixed up inside."

"If Kyle is attracted to you, what's preventing the two of you from getting together? The ghost of Jeff and Liz's affair?"

"You have to admit that it ended very badly for them. You even reminded me of that when you came over for Kyle's cast-signing party. You warned me then not to get romantically involved with Kyle. I thought I had everything under control, but boy, was I wrong. This is so much harder than I thought it would be. So much more complicated. You'd think it would be easy. I mean, Kyle and I are already friends, we already have so much in common. We've got a past together to build on, we like each other. You'd think those would all be ideal qualifications for starting a romantic relationship. Instead, here we are, afraid to go forward."

"Maybe that's your problem. You're afraid of repeating the mistakes Jeff and Liz made, and with good reason. After all, their situation was very similar to yours. But we don't really know what actually went on between Jeff and Liz. I mean, we know the eventual outcome, but we don't know what went wrong. Maybe that's something we should find out before automatically assuming that you and Kyle will come to the same end. After all, you and Kyle are two different people than Liz and Jeff."

"It's just that having Kyle's friendship is better than having nothing at all. I'd rather settle for that than have him out of my life completely."

Back at their apartment, Kyle was telling Jeff the same thing. "I don't want to risk losing Tory's friendship over this, whatever *this* is."

"*This* is trouble, buddy," Jeff retorted. "Take it from me. You don't want to get involved with friends. It makes things real messy when it's all over."

"Where did you and Liz go wrong?" Kyle asked with a friend's bluntness.

"I don't know. I've wondered about that a lot myself. Maybe we didn't have enough time to make the transition from friend to lover. Maybe we expected too much of each other."

Out in Brooklyn, Victoria was asking the same thing. "Where do you think she and Jeff went wrong? You were closer to Liz than I was. What do you think?"

"It's hard to say. I'm not sure Jeff is the kind of guy who'll ever settle down. He's afraid of growing up, of getting old, so he flies around from relationship to relationship because settling down is a sign of maturity, and that's something he's afraid of. I guess Liz thought she'd be the exception to the rule. You know, even though we've known the guys a long time, we've only been seeing them as friends, not as romantic partners. Jeff, Kyle, George—they've all got excellent qualifications to be friends. They're loyal, they're dependable. But only in their roles as friends. Change their roles and you're talking about another kettle of fish entirely."

"Okay, so Jeff's immature, and everyone knows George is a workaholic. What about Kyle?" Victoria asked.

"Kyle's an unknown. Unlike Jeff, he hasn't gone through a legion of women. He's devoted to his job the way George is, yet he's taken the time to get seriously involved with a few women. Do you remember that girl he was going with when we were at Columbia? Marlene something-or-other. He went with her for what—almost two years, wasn't it? As I recall, Kyle didn't appear to be particularly bitter or upset when they eventually broke up. They seemed to have parted amicably. After that he dated a lot of women until he found Anita. Then she was transferred to Cleveland, and their long-distance relationship ultimately ended. Again, Kyle didn't seem all that heartbroken."

"Is that good or bad?"

"How should I know?" Sue shrugged good-naturedly. "I'm just listing his love life as we've known it."

"Thanks, but that's an exercise I'd just as soon skip."

"Jealous?"

"You bet."

"You hid it well."

"I didn't realize what it was at the time, thankfully. And I was busy with my career and relationships of my own."

"None of which have been serious," Sue pointed out.

"They just never measured up to Kyle."

"You have got it bad, haven't you."

Victoria nodded morosely. "I was hoping I'd get over it. You know, like you get over a case of measles or chicken pox. But so far it hasn't worked out that way."

"What are you going to do?"

"I wish I knew."

* * *

On the other side of the East River, Jeff was asking Kyle the same question. "What are you going to do?"

"I wish I knew."

"I'm telling you, Kyle. Don't do it. Women change once you've gotten involved with them. They start getting ideas about settling down, starting a family, stuff like that. Look at Liz. She's always been ambitious about her career, a real go-getter. We'd known each other for years, but it turned out we didn't know each other at all. As a friend she'd never made demands on me, but as a lover she had all these expectations of how things should be between us. Suddenly she had our future mapped out for the next ten years. Marriage, buying a house, having kids." Jeff shook his head. "That's not where I'm coming from, and I didn't think it was where Liz was coming from, either. She said she thought she could change me. Now does that make sense? If she didn't like the way I was in the first place, she should never have gotten involved with me. Don't you agree?"

Kyle nodded.

"You know, it's a shame women can't think more like men," Jeff said. "It would sure make them a hell of a lot easier to figure out."

"Amen to that." But in the privacy of his own thoughts, Kyle admitted that he usually appreciated the differences between men and women, even if they did drive him to distraction. Especially the physical differences. And he'd been noticing those about Victoria more and more lately. Just the other day he'd run across a catalog of intimate feminine attire that she'd inadvertently left under a pile of *National Geographic*s on the coffee table. When he'd thumbed through it and found the order form missing, he couldn't help wondering if Tory had ordered something for herself and, if so, what? The possibilities were mind-boggling.

When Victoria returned home later that evening, she was surprised to find Jeff there. She hadn't known he was coming over, and after having just been discussing him with Sue she found it hard to act naturally toward him.

"So how's it going, Victoria?" Jeff asked her.

"Fine." Her voice was curt.

"Good. That's good." Sensing the sudden chill in the air, he prepared to make a hasty departure. "Uh, well, I think I'd better be getting along. Give me a call, Kyle, and let me know how things work out."

"What things?" Victoria demanded suspiciously, looking from Kyle to Jeff.

"Nothing in particular," Jeff said. "Just things in general. Jeez, are you jumpy tonight. Calm down."

He and Kyle exchanged a look that screamed masculine exasperation. They might as well have thrown up their hands and moaned, "Women!" Victoria resented the display of the boys sticking together.

It was hard, but she managed to keep her feelings to herself until Jeff had left. Then she confronted Kyle. "What were you and Jeff talking about?"

"Why the inquisition?" he countered. "You notice that I didn't ask you where you were tonight."

"I was at Sue's."

"What did you two talk about?"

She didn't answer.

"You see, it's not as much fun being on the receiving end, is it? And while we're playing twenty questions, why were you so rude to Jeff tonight?"

"I was not rude," she said vehemently.

"Yes, you were. You practically shoved him out of the apartment by giving him the cold shoulder."

"Frankly, I resented the man-to-man looks flying between you two at my expense. You know, Jeff can be incredibly chauvinistic sometimes. If that's a sample of what Liz had to put up with, it's no wonder she left."

Kyle immediately jumped to Jeff's defense. "What makes you think it was his fault and not hers?"

"So now you're blaming Liz? That's not fair."

"Your blaming Jeff isn't fair, either," he retorted.

"I should have known you'd side with him. You men always stick together!"

"And you woman always get so emotional!"

They glared at each other. Anger shimmered on the surface, but right beneath the anger was the attraction, and that was what they were both *really* fighting. The battle was just beginning.

Eight

In the privacy of her room, Victoria sat and brooded about their fight. She and Kyle never used to argue. But that had changed lately.

She was astute enough to know that, for her part, this latest argument hadn't been solely about Jeff or Liz. The subject had just been an excuse to air pent-up frustrations.

And she had plenty to feel frustrated about. The embrace they'd shared last night had proved to be impossible to forget. Every moment was indelibly etched in her mind, and this time no amount of willpower could erase the memory of what had happened.

As for Kyle, he was obviously intent on fighting any attraction he might feel toward her. Clearly it wasn't a feeling he welcomed in any way, shape or form. And that hurt her.

It shouldn't have surprised her. He probably didn't want to get involved with her for the same reasons she originally hadn't wanted to get involved with him. But for all her good intentions she hadn't been able to ignore her feelings. She couldn't turn her emotions on and off the way he seemed to be able to do.

What was he afraid of? That their friendship wouldn't survive once their romantic relationship had ended? Why did relationships have to end, anyway? Where was it written that people couldn't fall in love and stay together? Granted, she didn't know many contemporaries who'd had that luck, but surely it wasn't an impossibility. Rationally she knew there were happy couples around, couples who didn't break up and go their separate ways when something better came along. Couples who, with much work and effort, managed to live happily ever after.

She sat in a lotus position on her bed and reviewed her discussion with Sue about Kyle. How did he view relationships? Was he looking for something permanent? Why hadn't she ever thought to ask him these questions before she'd fallen in love with him?

She froze. The word shouldn't have scared her, but it did. Love. She'd said she loved Kyle before, but there was a world of difference between that kind of platonic love and the intense emotion she now felt.

And what about Kyle? What were his feelings for her? Reluctant attraction? An attraction that might only be caused by their proximity? The more she thought about it, the more convinced she became. After all, he was cooped up in the apartment day and night, and they were constantly thrown together. Her heart sank at the probable explanation. It made sense. He was only looking at her differently now because there was no one else to look at. Otherwise he'd have noticed her before this.

Her sudden attraction to him was even easier to understand. She'd had a crush on Kyle from the very beginning. It had just been lying there beneath the surface, like a seed in the desert waiting for the rain.

Wonderful. Unrequited love, infatuation—whatever you wanted to call it, she felt it and Kyle didn't. So now what should she do? Keep on pretending to act naturally? What else *could* she do? Confront him with the fact that she'd fallen for him? Aside from not reciprocating the feeling, he'd probably feel sorry for her. She cringed. No, she couldn't face that. Anything was preferable to that.

So she embarked on act two of this charade. Kyle played his role admirably, and an uneasy truce came into effect. Neither of them referred to their embrace, or their fight, or Liz or Jeff. In fact, there were more subjects she and Kyle were *not* talking about than subjects they *were*.

This went on for two days before it was brought to a halt by something larger than the two of them—the refrigerator. Actually, the appliance had been acting strangely for a few weeks now, and Kyle had called Mr. Dinkman about it before.

Victoria was the one who first discovered the latest problem. She went to the refrigerator to get her morning dose of grapefruit juice, only to open the door and have water trickle out onto the floor.

"Not today," she moaned. "Live a little longer, please." The appliance gave a shudder and simply quit. "Traitor!"

"Why are you talking to the refrigerator?" Kyle asked her.

She jumped guiltily. "I didn't realize you were there."

"With these crutches it's a little hard to sneak up on someone. You were totally engrossed in your discussion with the Frigidaire. Tell me, did it talk back?"

"Worse. It quit." Victoria quickly shut the door and reached for a roll of paper towels to wipe up the puddle of water on the floor.

Kyle tried to ignore the way her skirt rode up her legs—really he did. But it was to no avail. So he stopped feeling guilty and just enjoyed the view.

Unaware of Kyle's interest, Victoria finished soaking up the water and dumped the wad of dripping paper towels into the trash. "You'll have to call Mr. Dinkman again and have him either send a repairman out to fix it or get us a new one. Meanwhile we should try and keep the door shut to retain the coolness inside as long as possible. And we should eat what might spoil."

With that in mind, she opened the freezer, quickly grabbed a box of frozen blueberry pancakes and slammed it shut again. "We're having pancakes for breakfast. A dozen of them."

"Each?"

"No, split between the two of us."

"No problem."

She opened the freezer again and grabbed a few more boxes. "And sausages."

"Okay."

"And chocolate chocolate-chip ice cream."

"No way."

Victoria finished off the ice cream by herself.

Her day at work was as unproductive as the refrigerator was. Mr. Molenaar remained cool. Victoria's nerves were frayed by the continual strain of not knowing if or when her boss would again bring up the matter of her living with Kyle. Even though she knew he didn't have a leg to stand on as far as official policy went, she also knew that working under the disapproval of a supervisor was bound to have a negative impact. She'd even considered the possibility of transferring to another department but had decided that she needed more time to think about it before making any moves.

When she got home, there was still the problem of the refrigerator to contend with. "What did Mr. Dinkman say?" she asked Kyle.

"I got his answering machine. Five times. After I threatened to go over his head and contact the owners, he finally called back a few minutes ago. Claims he'll have someone out to look at it tomorrow."

"Good." She absently thumbed through her mail, throwing away the junk and leaving the bills unopened. She had enough problems for one night. "Meanwhile, we should use up the rest of the leftovers for dinner."

"Any idea of what exactly we have left over in there?"

"Sure. Milk, yogurt, grapefruit juice, last night's meat loaf, some zucchini..."

"That's all that's in there?"

"No. But it's all I can remember. Listing the contents of your refrigerator isn't as easy as you might think. It's your fridge too. What do you think is in there?"

"A six-pack of beer, a steak, a tub of Sue's curry dip and a jar of Cheez Whiz."

They finished up the meat loaf, the steak and the zucchini in an ad hoc meal that incorporated a few other items they ran across. As she sat at the table across from Kyle, Victoria's thoughts were centered on him and not on what she was eating. She looked at him through the screen of her lashes. It was an unobtrusive way to watch him without him knowing it—something she'd gotten quite good at doing. But then, she'd had a lot of practice at it.

Studying Kyle had become a frequent pastime of hers. One would have thought that, having known him as long as she had, she'd have seen all there was to see. But then she'd been looking at him with the eyes of a friend, not the eyes of a woman who was attracted to him.

She noticed so much more now. Small things, endearing things, sexy things. The way he held his knife and fork, the way he combed an impatient hand through his hair when he was working, the way he suddenly smiled in the middle of a sentence. These were all simple actions that absolutely fascinated her. They were all sure signs that she had it bad, and that wasn't good.

Her wistful gaze bumped into his curious one. She'd been staring at him without realizing it. She recovered quickly. "I've been meaning to ask you if you have any plans for Thanksgiving this year. It's only two weeks away."

"Actually, I got a letter from my younger brother Rick a few days ago," Kyle said. "He'll be in town over the holiday and wondered if we could get together."

"That'll be nice. It's been a while since you've seen him, hasn't it?"

Kyle nodded. "With me traveling so much and him working in Alaska, it's been pretty hard getting together."

"He's in the construction business, too, isn't he?"

"Yes, and he seems to be doing real well. He's even building his own place, out near Homer, I think. Of course, it's seasonal work, but he goes south during the winters. The company he now works for has other offices in Seattle and San Diego, as well as Anchorage."

"You know the last time I saw Rick was at our graduation from Columbia," Victoria said. "He was still in high school then. I hope he stays in town long enough for me to meet him again."

"You're going up to Vermont for the holiday?"

She nodded. "I'll be going to my parents Thanksgiving morning and flying back Friday evening."

"Everyone showing up for the occasion as usual?"

Victoria grinned. "That's right. Both of my brothers will be there. It's my parents' turn to host the annual event, so all the aunts and uncles and cousins are coming to our house. Most of them live in the area, but one of my cousins is flying in from Texas with her husband and their new baby."

"It must make quite a crowd."

"I think my mom's planning on dinner for thirty. What about your parents?"

"They're taking their annual cruise."

"Where to this time?"

"From Miami to San Diego via the Panama Canal. Not as exotic as that China cruise they took last year, but my dad wants to stick closer to home this year."

"There's no doubt about it, wanderlust runs in your family," she declared. "You O'Reillys are always off roaming the globe. Compared to you, we Winterses are real homebodies. The farthest my parents have ever traveled is here to New York, and they couldn't wait to get back home. Both of my brothers are still in Vermont. I live the farthest away."

"I may do a lot of traveling, but I do have roots," Kyle pointed out. "I've had this apartment for seven years now."

"That's more than I can claim. In the nine years I've been in the city I've lived in six different apartments, with at least as many different roommates."

"None of whom were nearly as congenial as I am."

She gave him a look that spoke volumes and changed the subject. "How about dessert? We have cookies and whipping cream."

Kyle looked askance at the metal container she set on the table. "That's not whipping cream."

"Sure it is, says so on the can."

"It's had something strange done to it," he maintained.

She shook the can, turned it upside down and pushed the nozzle. Very carefully she created a series of whipped-cream rosettes around the perimeter of her Oreo cookie. She paused for a moment to admire her masterpiece before popping it into her mouth.

When Kyle tried decorating his cookie, he misdirected the nozzle and ended up spraying his shirt front.

Victoria couldn't help herself. He looked so stunned that she had to laugh. "Now you've gone and done it." She stood up and grabbed a few paper napkins from the center of the table. Bracing one hand on his shoulder, she prepared to wipe the whipping cream from his flannel shirt. But the moment she touched him, he jerked away from her.

"Don't!" He grabbed the paper napkin from her numb fingers. "I'll do it myself."

She backed away, incredibly hurt by what she saw as yet another rejection. He'd never jerked away from her like that before, and she could think of only one reason why he'd done it now. He didn't want her touching him. It was that plain and simple. She died a little inside.

Seeing the pain in her eyes, Kyle realized what he'd done. "I'm sorry, I didn't mean—"

She shook her head and blinked back the tears. She'd reached her limit. This time she couldn't pretend that nothing had happened.

"This isn't working," she said in a choked voice.

"Don't worry about the shirt."

"I'm not talking about the damn shirt! I'm talking about us," she said, then immediately corrected herself. "About me." There was no *us* in this instance. *She* was the one with the problem. "I can't keep playing this game anymore."

"What game?"

"The one where I'm just a friend who's helping you out by pretending to be your girlfriend. The one where you kiss me as if you mean it and then forget all about it and treat me like your sister. The one where I pretend nothing has changed when *everything* has. You remember when you first got here with your broken ankle? You said that you knew things wouldn't get sticky with us living together. Well, you were wrong. They have gotten sticky. Not because of you, because of me. Because I'm attracted to you in ways that have nothing to do with friendship. But you've made it very clear that you don't feel anything but friendship for me—you never have and you never will."

"Tory, that's not true."

"What's not true?"

"That I feel nothing but friendship for you."

"Now you're just trying to make me feel better."

"No, I'm not. I pulled away from you just now because—"

"Because you can't stand to have me touch you anymore," she said.

"No, because I want you to touch me, want it too much."

"I don't believe you."

He abruptly tugged her down onto his lap. "Then believe this," he muttered. And then he kissed her.

Nine

He took her breath away. His kiss was no teasing caress, it was the fervent declaration of a man who'd reached the end of his patience. It spoke of raw need and blatant hunger.

At first Victoria was too stunned to respond. His mouth was exploring the contours of hers as if she were more essential to him than the very air he breathed. She was caught completely off guard.

Sensing that, he broke off the kiss long enough to mutter, "Now do you believe me?"

Astonished by his unexpected display of passion, she could only blink dazedly and nod.

"Good," he whispered huskily before kissing her again.

Captured between his caressing hands and his mouth, she had nowhere to go. She could only move closer, and she did that gladly. This time she returned his kiss with equal enthusiasm. Sliding her arms around his neck, she melted against him. Now she could feel his heart pounding against her breast, and its tempo was as hectic as her own.

His hold on her was possessive, as was hers on him. His hands made themselves familiar with every part of her, from the nape of her neck to the curve of her bottom. The khaki material of his slacks couldn't hide the fact that he was aroused. Her own excitement was evident in the way her breasts pressed eagerly against his chest.

Enthralled, Kyle pulled her even closer. His hand slid from her back and trailed over her lower rib cage to hover near the sloping curve of her breast. He paused, as if giving her the opportunity to protest. She didn't. She wanted him to touch her, and he did. The pleasure he created with the stroke of his hand was incredibly exciting. She felt wild and free. Wanting to share her elation, she reached up to blindly undo the buttons of his shirt. With shaking hands she pushed aside the material in favor of the bronzed warmth of his skin.

Kyle returned the favor, unbuttoning her blouse halfway and slipping his hand inside to caress her enticing softness. Their embrace was in danger of escalating out of control when it all abruptly came to an end as Kyle broke off their heated kiss with a shudder and a groan of pain.

"What is it...what happened?" she asked, disoriented.

"My ankle, I just hit it against the table leg."

"Are you okay?"

"No."

"What can I do to help?"

"Kiss me again."

She did, but it was over much too quickly for Kyle's satisfaction.

"We need to talk," she told him, preparing to get up from his lap.

Kyle was clearly reluctant to let her go. Coaxing her back to him, he began nuzzling her neck with his lips. "Why can't you talk right where you are?"

She shivered with pleasure. "Because I can't think straight when you're holding me like this." She moved away while she still had the willpower to do so.

He sighed and let her go.

She didn't go far. For one thing, she didn't trust her shaky legs to hold her up. For another, she didn't want to be far from Kyle. So she sank onto a nearby dining room chair, still within touching distance, yet out of temptation's way.

Kyle was the one who asked the question that was on both of their minds. "So now what do we do?"

"I'm not sure." She drew in an unsteady breath and shakily did up the buttons he'd undone. "I'm still trying to get used to the fact that you feel the same way, too. I didn't have a clue."

Kyle made no move to refasten his shirt. He kind of liked the hungry way she looked at him. "You mean you didn't notice the way I kept playing the blues on my harmonica at night?"

She'd noticed, and she'd spent several restless nights herself mulling over the possible meaning behind it. "I thought maybe it was a sign that you were tired of having me around."

"Wrong." He reached out and gently touched her cheek with his fingers. "I loved having you around, but it was affecting me in ways I hadn't anticipated. *You* were affecting me in ways I hadn't anticipated. And I wasn't sure if you felt the same way."

"Couldn't you tell from the way I kissed you?"

"It could have been part of the act to fool Angelica."

"She was never even around when I kissed you, and besides, I'm not that good an actress. It was real. It *is* real."

"Why didn't you say something earlier?"

"I didn't want to embarrass you by 'going all sentimental' on you—your words, remember?"

Kyle nodded ruefully. "Little did I know that one day I'd live to regret those words."

"Do you really regret them? How can you be sure that what you're feeling isn't just...I don't know...some kind of artificial attraction? After all, you've been stuck here with me for a month now. Maybe you're just experiencing an emotional transference. How can you be sure?"

He leaned over and put his finger over her lips, effectively silencing her. "I know," he said softly. "I'm sure."

"I don't want us to end up the way Liz and Jeff did," she murmured huskily.

"Neither do I."

"Do you really think it was all Liz's fault?" The question had been preying on her mind.

"No, I never did. You're referring to that argument we had the other night, aren't you?"

She nodded.

"But then, we weren't really arguing about Jeff and Liz at all, were we? It was just an excuse to release the tension that was building between us."

"That's pretty perceptive of you," she said.

"I can't take all the credit. Sue came up with the idea, and it sounded logical to me."

"You talked to Sue about this...about us?"

He nodded. "Didn't you?"

She nodded. "What did Sue tell you?"

"She didn't break any confidences, if that's what's worrying you. She never let on that you might be attracted to me. But then, I didn't exactly let on to her that I was attracted to you."

Victoria sighed. "Relationships can sure get complicated, can't they?"

Kyle nodded. "Jeff and I were talking about that very subject when he was over here the other night."

"Oh, so you and Jeff were talking about us? I thought you were. Did you reach any conclusions?"

"Nope. How about you and Sue?"

Victoria shook her head.

"So where do we go from here?" he asked.

"I think we need to take our time and not rush into anything. I think maybe that's where Jeff and Liz went wrong, they went from being friends to being lovers without a period of adjustment. I don't want us to rush into anything we might later regret, so let's just take things one step at a time and see how it goes. What do you think?"

"I think it sounds frustrating but probably sensible."

Victoria would have preferred sensual over sensible any day, but what they shared was too important to risk damaging in haste.

"You're worth waiting for," he added softly.

"So are you," she replied with a seductive smile.

From that moment on they spent every free moment together, making Victoria realize how much they'd been avoiding each other lately. And every evening Kyle played the same song on his harmonica. It didn't take Victoria long to recognize the melody. It was Carly Simon's song "Anticipation."

He was doing it deliberately, she knew that. And knowing it only increased their shared anticipation, which was why he'd played the song in the first place! Victoria had always been the kind who liked looking forward to things—vacations, Christmas, a carton of chocolate chocolate-chip ice cream. Shaking a present and imagining what was inside before opening it was half the fun.

They both knew it was only a matter of time. The waiting seemed to make the eventual outcome even sweeter. During those days everything seemed new. The sparks between them added a special radiance to the most mundane of things. The sun seemed to shine brighter, even when it was cloudy. Victoria found herself smiling at the most inane things. Even her boss's attitude temporarily failed to aggravate her. It was almost as if she were operating under some powerful shield that filtered out the bad and allowed only the good to come through. Life had never felt so wonderful.

Even a chore like vacuuming was suddenly filled with a world of new possibilities. Kyle was sitting on the couch, working. Global had been sending material over by messenger on almost a daily basis, and Victoria couldn't help wishing wistfully for some of the attention he was bestowing upon those papers. He was so engrossed in his work that he didn't notice how close she was getting. Upon request he did lift his feet as she ran the vacuum over the rug, but that was the only outward sign that he was aware of her presence. When she added the hand-held attachment and began doing the upholstery on the couch, Kyle stayed right where he was.

"If you're not going to move, I'll just have to vacuum around you," she told him. And she did just that, but she couldn't resist vacuuming him, too.

Victoria shrieked with delighted surprise as Kyle growled and immediately tugged her across his lap so that he could kiss her. Obviously he hadn't been as oblivious as she'd thought! Their kiss began with laughter, but it soon grew more serious as Kyle mimicked the suction motion of the vacuum with which she'd teased him. He skillfully, teasingly sucked on her lower lip, drawing her tongue out of hiding. Things were getting very heated when a sudden screeching sound drove them apart. It was the abandoned vacuum cleaner hose, which had plastered itself to the back of the couch, thereby triggering a warning signal.

Victoria had a few warning signals of her own going off. Time was running out. It wouldn't be long now.

Only one thing marred her happiness that week—the appearance of Angelica. Victoria came home from work on Wednesday and literally bumped into the other woman in the apartment building's small lobby. It looked as though Angelica had tears in her eyes. Victoria barely had time to register that fact before Angelica rushed past her and hurried out to her waiting limo.

All the way up in the elevator Victoria weighed the pros and cons of asking Kyle directly or waiting to see if he brought up Angelica's visit himself. By the time she entered the apartment she'd opted for the direct approach.

"I saw Angelica downstairs," Victoria said as she took off her coat and hung it up. "What happened?"

"I had a talk with her." Kyle was pacing the living room floor—a difficult task for a man on crutches. "Did you know that she's the one who told your boss about us?"

"I had my suspicions, but how did you find out?"

"She told me."

"She just came out and confessed?"

"No," he admitted, somewhat grimly. "It came out in the course of our conversation."

Victoria tried to lighten the atmosphere by saying, "That must have been some conversation the two of you had."

"I think we cleared things up."

She sat on the couch and patted the cushion next to her invitingly. Kyle took the hint and sat down beside her.

"It looked to me like she'd been crying," Victoria noted quietly.

He heard the empathy in her voice. "Only you would feel sorry for someone who's caused you so much trouble."

"What about you? Will you get into trouble at work because of what you said today?"

"I can take care of myself," he said.

Victoria remembered Sue saying that about Kyle—that he was able to look after himself. That he could be hard when he needed to be, but only with people who deserved it.

"I feel badly about all the trouble she's stirred up for you at work," he said. "And I feel partly to blame. After all, if I hadn't dragged you into this mess by asking for your help, you would never have gotten involved with Angelica."

"It's not your fault," she said reassuringly.

"The least I can do is talk to your boss."

"And what will you tell him? We are living together and we're not married. That's all he seems to be worried about."

"I'll think of something."

"You might just make things worse."

"You're not the only one who can be diplomatic, you know. I caused you this trouble, I'll fix it," he stubbornly maintained.

"I'd rather you just let sleeping dogs lie."

"So your boss is a sleeping dog, hmmm? I've dealt with the type before."

"So have I," she retorted. "Believe me, there's no way to change Mr. Molenaar's mind about this. Once he's got something set in his mind, that's it."

"Who said anything about changing his mind? I'm just going to clarify the situation for him a bit, that's all."

"It's none of his business."

"That's true, but the tension at work is getting to you, and that's my business. Let me try. I promise you I won't make it worse for you."

"We'll talk about it later," she replied.

They said no more about it, but Victoria noticed a difference in Mr. Molenaar's behavior toward her the next afternoon. His disapproval had dissipated, and that made her suspicious. She confronted Kyle as soon as she got home. "Okay, what did you say to him?"

"What are you talking about?" he asked with a boyish innocence that didn't fool her for one minute.

"I'm talking about your phone call to my boss. You did talk to him today, didn't you?"

"What makes you think that?"

"Because he's not treating me like a leper anymore."

"Glad to hear it. Then what's the problem?"

"The problem is that I didn't give you permission to go over my head and talk to him, Kyle. You should have talked to me first."

"I did. Last night, remember?"

"And I said I'd think about it, remember?"

"And now that you've thought about it, wasn't it a good idea?"

She shook her head and tried to stifle her grin at his quick comeback. But she soon became serious again. "What did you tell him?"

"Nothing you wouldn't want me to." And that was all he would say about the matter, despite her best efforts to get him to elaborate.

"Do you think you can kiss the story out of me?" he asked her later that evening as they cuddled on the couch and she asked him again about the phone call.

"I don't know. Can I?" She brushed her mouth across his, placing a kiss in between each word.

"No." He nibbled on her bottom lip. "But you're welcome to keep trying!"

She was still trying the next night. They were sitting in front of the TV, their feet propped up on the coffee table, a bowl of popcorn in Victoria's lap, as they prepared to watch a special Friday-night presentation of the silent movie classic *The Thief of Baghdad*.

Kyle had set her off by saying, "Did you know that Walter loves to play darts?"

"Walter who?"

"Your boss, Walter Molenaar. Who else would I be talking about? When he found out I play, too, he said we'd have to get together someday and play a game."

Personally, Victoria thought that Kyle was the one playing games, but, strangely enough, she didn't mind. Trying to finagle the truth out of him was turning out to be so much fun that she'd just as soon he didn't tell her the whole story just yet.

She was still amazed at how well they meshed together, not just physically, but emotionally, as well. Their embraces had the personal experience of their friendship and the new excitement of their desire. That meant that she knew exactly where Kyle liked having his back rubbed, right down to the knotted ligament in his right shoulder. It also meant that when she gave him a back rub she was now free to touch him in ways that had nothing to do with friendship, and everything to do with enticement.

She wasn't the only one eagerly exploring the new avenues of their relationship. Kyle indulged himself fully, as well. One thing he loved to do was run his fingers through her hair whenever she rested her head on his shoulder, which was quite frequently. She'd teasingly asked him if he was making a wish and hoping she'd turn into a brunette. He'd framed her face with his hands and kissed her with hungry directness. "I like you just the way you are," he said firmly.

They both knew *like* meant *want* and *need*. It was clear from the increasing intimacy of their kisses and embraces. They were all building up to one thing, the ultimate act of love. And it was love for Victoria. She loved Kyle with every fiber of her being. But then, she'd had longer to get used to the idea. It had been sitting in her heart all along, just waiting for the light of his attention to make it burst into life. She felt that Kyle's feelings for her must be more complicated, but she had great faith that things would work out between them. They had more going for them than most couples. They'd make it work.

"You're frowning," Kyle noted. "What's the matter?"

"Nothing." She distracted him by pointing to the TV. "Look, the movie's starting. Now remember, this is a silent movie, so you're not going to be able to close your eyes and fill in the story just by listening to it."

"Since when do I watch TV with my eyes closed?" he demanded with pretended outrage.

"Since I've known you."

Suddenly the word known took on new connotations, held out new promise. They shared a look that said it all—the excitement, the hunger, the promise of fulfillment. As if to echo their feelings, the sensual sound of Rimsky-Korsakov's *Scheherazade* filled the room with its richness. The music was the perfect background, not only for the movie but also for what was happening between them.

As they watched the story unfold, Victoria couldn't help comparing Kyle to the swashbuckling hero, Douglas Fairbanks, Sr. For one thing, the two men shared a similar daredevil gleam in their eyes. Then, of course, there were the matching wide shoulders, trim waists, muscular chests. Victoria felt her temperature rising.

When she'd suggested watching the movie, she'd had no idea that it would be so sensual. After all, it had been filmed in 1924! But that hadn't stopped Douglas Fairbanks from appearing naked to the waist in most scenes. It was strange, but she found the princess's veils and the hero's romantic kisses more suggestive than most R-rated movies, which proved once again the power of suggestion.

The story was vividly told, with special effects that were well ahead of their time. But aside from the adventure and the showmanship, there was the simple tale of an ordinary man's love for a princess and his quest to win her heart. The trials and tribulations he had to go through were many, but in the end the hero saved the day and whisked the lovely princess off on a magical flying carpet.

Victoria had felt the tension building between herself and Kyle from the first kiss shown on the screen. A mood had been set. Exotic places, magical times—romance.

It began with her fingers tangling with Kyle's in the popcorn bowl. As the excitement on the screen progressed, so, too, did the excitement between them. Inspired by the story, Kyle brought her hand to his lips and kissed the butter from her fingertips. He made her feel as desirable as the princess in her ivory tower and silken veils. They didn't take their eyes from the screen, which made the interplay between them even more evocative.

As the hero fought off an enormous sea monster, Victoria was fighting to keep her breathing stable. Kyle's kisses had slowly but surely progressed from her fingertips down to the ultrasensitive skin between her fingers, where he teased her with flicks of his tongue. He moved on, nibbling on the mound at the base of her thumb. He kissed every inch of her palm and then stroked his tongue across the racing pulse at her wrist. Victoria had never had so much attention paid to her hand before, and she realized what a terrible deprivation that had been. Her entire arm hummed from erogenous zones she hadn't even known she'd had.

When she thought she couldn't bear the pleasure a moment longer, Kyle expanded his sensual explorations from her wrist up along the inside of her arm. The filmy material of her oversize Indian cotton shirt suddenly took on the nuances of a Middle Eastern caftan. The very subtleness of his approach was what made it so sexy. Pleasure like this wasn't meant to be hurried, it was meant to be savored slowly and shared.

When Kyle had finished taking her breath away with secret kisses placed along the length of her arm, she returned the favor with a sensual exploration of her own. His fingers were just as slick with melted butter as hers had been, and he was just as susceptible to the touch of her lips on his hand. She repeated every move he'd made. Every swipe of his tongue was mimicked by hers and often elaborated on with stunning success. She ran the edge of her teeth across the base of his thumb and felt the tension in him grow.

He used his free hand to steal a touch here and there. Smoothing her hair from her neck, tracing the curve of her ear, caressing her shoulder—innocent touches with the naughtiest of intentions. It was only a matter of time before his hand reached her leg and the surprisingly sensitive place behind her knee. The stretchy black leggings she wore had been chosen as much for comfort as for looks, and Victoria had had no idea that they would so magnify his touch. She caught her breath as his fingers continued their restless explorations, softly stealing ever higher, beneath the hip-length hem of her shirt, to skim her thigh.

Unable to stay still a moment longer, Victoria shifted her leg. Kyle transformed the fitful movement into an erotic embrace as he guided her outstretched leg on top of his. His knee fit snugly into the back of hers. She used her bare heel to rub the tension from his calf muscles. Her leggings and his slacks seemed to be having a love affair of their own, the two materials creating an explosive friction.

By the time the movie ended, so, too, had their patience.

"Is this the part where I sweep you up into my arms and carry you to the bedroom?" he asked in a husky growl before remembering his broken ankle.

"It's the part where I take you by the hand and lead you to happiness," she replied with a sultry smile that Scheherazade would have been proud of.

Kyle swore at his crutches, but he moved with a speed that surprised her. He was standing before she was. "Well, what are you waiting for?" he demanded with a devilish grin.

Then they were in her bedroom. The double bed, with its abundance of jewel-toned pillows, seemed to have taken on the appearance of an Arabian fantasy.

"Are you sure?" he asked, even as his hands slipped beneath her shirt to caress her bare back.

"I'm sure. Are you?"

"Am I what?" he asked in a distracted murmur.

"Sure."

"I'm positive."

There was no more talk. Words were replaced by sighs and muttered groans of pleasure. Her oversize shirt floated to the floor, soon followed by his. Her stretchy leggings were easier to dispense with than his slacks, which got caught on his cast. Kyle's frustration turned to delight as Victoria took the opportunity to slide her hands down his legs and take care of the hang-up herself. His slacks provided no opposition to her wiles, and neither did he.

Their lovemaking took on a faster, more urgent tempo as needs clamored to be satisfied. Their kiss reflected the increasing intensity between them. Her parted lips conveyed an invitation that he readily accepted. His tongue tangled with hers in an ageless rhythm indicative of what was yet to come.

Meanwhile, his hands were busy freeing her breasts from the wispy confines of her bra. Kyle no longer had to wonder if she'd ordered anything from that catalog of intimate apparel. He recognized the sinfully silky little nothings she was wearing. They'd been on the cover of the catalog, but in his opinion the model hadn't done them justice. Victoria did. She filled the thin silk to perfection, and she fit into the palm of his hand with equal ease. He undid the front fastening of her bra. She was creamy soft and temptingly warm. Her bare skin gleamed in the darkness, beckoning him closer. When she shivered, he warmed her with his hands and aroused her with his mouth.

Victoria speared her fingers through his hair and held him close as he practiced his masculine magic on her. His cajoling tongue swirled seductively, and his gentle teeth tugged erotically. The tips of her breasts became rosy from the lavish attention. An aching need welled up from deep within her, from the secret places that longed for his touch. She arched upward, her back leaving the mattress as she twisted hungrily beneath him.

Her movements drove Kyle onward. He kissed the moan of pleasure from her lips and slid his hands around her waist to the small of her back. So adeptly did he move that she wasn't even aware of what he'd done until she felt him there, right where she wanted him to be. The stimulating warmth of his hand replaced the triangular silken veil of her underwear as he covered her heat with the palm of his hand.

Passions flared. As skillfully as he'd done with her, she slid her fingers beneath the elastic waistband of his white cotton briefs and peeled them away. Any doubts that his ankle might inhibit his mobility were discarded at this stage as he moved against her with mounting desire.

Now, when they pressed close, there was nothing to separate them. Nothing to disguise the need. His skin was hot to the touch, as was hers. The intimate promises he whispered to her made her warmer still. And when his fingers followed through on the promises he'd made, the flames almost burned her. His caresses were bold but infinitely tender and darkly exciting. Pulses of sheer delight shot through her. She blossomed and flowered for him.

Her breath was coming in breathless little pants as he gently brushed the dampened strands of hair away from her face. "Are you protected, or should I—"

"It's taken care of," she whispered, somewhat shyly.

He kissed every inch of her flushed face.

Wanting to share her pleasure, she ran her hands over his body with eager anticipation and loving appreciation. She touched him as he'd touched her, tenderly, intimately. His ragged groan warned her that his self-control was weakening and his desire was growing.

He turned onto his side and pulled her with him. Sliding one hand beneath her knee, he positioned her leg so that it was draped across his hip. Once again his skillful fingers aroused her to the point of no return, confirming that she was ready for him. Unable to hold out any longer, Victoria boldly guided him to her.

Kyle whispered her name and took what she so sensuously offered. His entry was slow and sure as he introduced himself to her in heated stages, making sure that she could accept all that he had to give. She fit him like a glove, sheathing him deep within. He'd never experienced such utter bliss.

Awed by the intensity of what they were sharing, Victoria opened her eyes and watched him. His face was etched with passion, his blue eyes dark with desire. This was the way she'd dreamed of seeing him, of being with him. It felt so good to finally be completely joined with him. She wanted to tell him, but there were no words. Words were superfluous at that point, anyway. Physical expression was much more rewarding.

He rocked against her, and she needed no further urging to match his rhythm with her own. They moved together in an ancient undulation of give-and-take. Her hands clutched the small of his back as the rising tempo of his thrusts created an incredibly erotic friction. The deeper his penetration, the deeper her satisfaction, until the ripples of pleasure grew into powerful contractions. Her climax fueled his own, and with a final groan of pleasure he stiffened and then collapsed in her arms.

They both lay there, overwhelmed by the enormity of their satisfaction. Victoria might not have had much experience to compare it with, but she knew nothing could be better than what they'd just shared.

She was wrong. The next time *was* even better.

Ten

"Your feet are cold!" Kyle exclaimed.

"Is that all the thanks I get for bringing you breakfast in bed?"

"Breakfast? Tory, it's two in the afternoon."

"Well, if you're going to get picky about it—" She acted as if she were going to take the wicker bed tray away.

He hastily reconsidered. "No, I'm sure it must be time for breakfast somewhere in the world...Hawaii, maybe."

"Sounds like a nice place to have breakfast. Lots of warm tropical breezes." She picked up a piece of buttered toast and began nibbling on it. "It's sleeting outside here."

"All the more reason to stay in bed."

"I couldn't agree with you more. Here, try the bacon. It's done just right."

She held out the crispy slice to him. He ate half of it in one bite, and she popped what was left into her mouth.

"Mmm, good," he mumbled as he ate.

"There's also yogurt..."

He made a face at her.

"...scrambled eggs and coffee."

He sat up and showed more interest. "That sounds better." He dug in with gusto.

"I never knew you liked my scrambled eggs so much," she teased him as he devoured the entire plateful.

"After going without food for fourteen hours, even your scrambled eggs look good."

"Ungrateful wretch," she retorted in mock indignation.

"Is that any way to talk to the man in your bed?"

"It is when he insults me."

"I didn't insult you, I insulted your scrambled eggs. You're perfect, the eggs aren't."

"Weren't. They're all gone. And I admit I may have had my mind on other things while I was cooking them."

"Really? What other things?" he asked, even though he already had a good idea. He could read it in her eyes.

And she could see that he was already anticipating her answer, which was why she decided to prevaricate a bit longer. "Oh, nothing important."

"Nothing important!" he exclaimed with a comical wounded expression.

"You think the weather's important?"

"You were thinking about the weather?"

She nodded. "That and..."

"And?" he repeated eagerly, playing the game as well as she was.

"Other things."

"Like?"

"Like how I can't think straight when you kiss me. Like how I couldn't wait to get back here in bed with you." She leaned forward and gave him a quick kiss. "What about you? What were you thinking about before I brought in breakfast?"

"That I was hungry."

"That's it?"

He frowned as he pretended an attempt at recollection. "No, there was something else.... What was it now?"

"The mind's starting to go already?"

Their friendship gave them the ability to share this kind of teasing banter, just as their recent lovemaking had given them the opportunity to explore new ways of sharing.

It was the memory of all the sharing they'd done throughout the night and well into the morning that brought a devilish grin to Kyle's face. Setting aside the tray so that it was safely out of harm's way, he reached out with lightning swiftness and tugged Victoria into his arms. She landed with a surprised "Oh!" in the middle of his bare chest.

"I was also thinking how good my shirt looks on you," he told her in a husky growl. She'd only done up half the buttons on the shirt so that it revealed the shadowy valley between her breasts and a generous expanse of bare thigh. There was something intrinsically sexy about a woman wearing nothing but her man's shirt, Kyle thought to himself, but there was something even more irresistible about seeing this particular woman dressed this way.

Tory had the look of a woman who'd been well loved. Her blond hair was tousled from the way he'd run his fingers through it. Her lips were ripe and slightly swollen from his kisses, her face still flushed. And her eyes—her eyes looked at him with a sirenlike sultriness that made his blood pressure, among other things, rise.

Unable to resist any longer, he reached for her.

"If you like this shirt on me so much, why are you taking it off me?" she inquired with a delightful show of perplexity.

"Because it's in my way."

"All you had to do was ask, Kyle. You know I'd give you the shirt off my back." She smiled and whipped it off.

They did manage to get out of bed for dinner, but they didn't eat it until eight. It was still sleeting outside, and the wet streets reflected the smeared images of streetlights. Inside the apartment it was toasty-warm. *Everything I want is right within these four walls,* Victoria thought to herself with lazy contentment. They'd finished eating and were now snuggled together, spoon fashion, on the living room couch. His arms circled her as he drew her shoulders back against his chest.

It was warm in his arms and she nestled closer, leaning her head back until it rested against his cheek. "You make a really nice backrest, you know that?"

"Nice to know I come in handy for something." His arms were crossed between her breasts, his hands resting on her shoulders.

"You come in handy for a lot of things. I couldn't have gotten that jar of apple sauce open without you."

He moved one hand, slipping it under her sweatshirt. "That's not all you couldn't have done without me."

"I know," she murmured. "And you're so good at everything you do."

"Mmm, so are you." He nuzzled the sensitive juncture between her ear and the nape of her neck.

"So what would you like to do tonight?" she asked him.

He slowly turned her until she was facing him. One look said it all. He wanted her. There. Now.

She smiled, slowly, seductively. "I'd like that, too."

She didn't just like it, she loved it, just as she loved him.

They spent the entire weekend together in a magical interlude out of time. Sunday found them sprawled out on the newly made bed, bickering over who got to read which section of *The New York Times* first. They were presently having a tug-of-war over the highly coveted arts and leisure section.

"Get your hands off," she scolded him. "You've got the sports section, you don't need this, too. You can't read both at the same time. Stop being so greedy."

"You didn't seem to mind my being greedy last night."

"That's different. You weren't hoarding the newspaper then."

"I'm not hoarding it now," he denied.

"Then you won't mind if I take *The New York Times Magazine*, the travel section, the book reviews and—"

He snatched the papers back out of her seeking hands. "Now who's being greedy?"

"How about if I trade you the Business section for Arts and Leisure?"

"Throw in The Week in Review and you've got a deal."

"You're a tough negotiator."

"Yeah, but I got a heart of gold."

They exchanged papers.

"Do you believe this?" He pulled out a color advertising supplement from Bloomingdale's. "Everybody's advertising for Christmas already."

"I know. Some of the displays have been up in the stores since Halloween."

"I haven't even been in a store since Halloween. I suppose you're already done with your Christmas shopping." He sounded resigned.

She nodded complacently. "Finished it in October."

"You only do that because it drives me crazy."

"No, I only do *this*—" she ran her fingernails down his bare back "—because it drives you crazy."

"How do you expect me to concentrate on the sports page when you do that?"

"Bothers you, does it?" she asked with seductive innocence.

"Let me show you how much." He growled and pinned her to the mattress.

The newspaper was completely forgotten.

They finally got dressed late Sunday afternoon, but only because Victoria had a craving for tollhouse chocolate-chip pan cookies. When Kyle decided to join her in the kitchen, she put him to work stirring the dough.

"I saw that, Kyle! If you keep swiping the cookie batter, there won't be enough left for the cookies. You're worse than a little kid, you know that?"

"I was just testing, making sure it tastes good. And it does. What's that?" he questioned suspiciously as she added more ingredients.

"Chopped dried apricots and cashews." Seeing his disbelieving frown, she said, "It'll taste wonderful. Trust me."

He did until he saw what she had in the next measuring cup. "You're going to ruin perfectly good chocolate-chip cookies by putting granola in them?"

"I'm going to make them even better. You'll see."

He didn't believe her until he'd tasted the finished product.

"Well, do you approve?"

He nodded.

"See, I know what I'm doing."

They watched *60 Minutes* and then changed the station, at Victoria's insistence, to watch a popular situation comedy on NBC. The clock was creeping toward eight forty-five when Kyle suddenly announced, "Time for bed!"

She followed him into her bedroom. "Now that you mention it, I am a little sleepy," she replied, feigning a yawn. She gathered her nightgown and went into the bathroom to change, leaving a disgruntled Kyle behind.

By the time she returned, he'd taken off all his clothes and climbed into bed. "Are you serious? You're really sleepy? Isn't it a little early?" he inquired with a meaningful glance at the clock on her bedside table.

"You know what they say..." She grinned and pushed him back onto the mattress. "Early to bed..." She ran her hands over his bare chest. "...and early to rise..." She touched him intimately. "...makes a man healthy..." She kissed his left shoulder. "...wealthy..." She kissed his right shoulder. "...and wise." She kissed his mouth.

And with wisdom came knowledge of the most erotically intimate sort as they made love to each other yet again.

Her hands, his body...his hands, her body—these were seductive combinations. Together they approached the ultimate peak and then, in a shattering burst of simultaneous passion, the final throes of ecstasy.

They lay together, arms and limbs still entwined, as the lingering vibrations of satiated desire shook them both.

It was then that Victoria heard herself whisper the words that had been going through her head. "I love you, Kyle. I love you!"

They were still intimately connected, and she could feel the change come over him immediately. He withdrew from her, both physically and emotionally. The expression on his face was one of such nonplussed discomfiture that she quickly retracted the words. "I didn't mean that."

Now he wore his poker face.

She was floundering now. "I mean, I did mean it in that I love you as a friend—" That didn't sound right, either.

"Forget it." His voice was rough. "Sometimes it's better to stop while you're ahead."

"Kyle—"

"Tory, believe me, this is one of those times when the best words are no words at all."

Even though they didn't speak of the incident again, it remained in the back of Victoria's mind for the next three days. She tried to tell herself that she was imagining the awkwardness between them. After all, every evening they still made love with a passion as forceful and as ardent as before. But it was the other times, the times spent at ease with one another in companionable silence, that she missed.

She hadn't meant to pressure Kyle by telling him she loved him, it had just sort of slipped out. The words weren't important, anyway. Kyle didn't have to tell her, he showed her that he loved her. She could wait for the rest, and she refused to allow her embarrassment to mar the time they had together.

She'd been looking forward to the trip home to Vermont for Thanksgiving, but that had been before she and Kyle had become lovers. Now she missed him already, and she hadn't even left yet. She checked her bedroom to make sure she'd packed everything into her overnight case.

"Bernie just called up, he's got a cab waiting downstairs," Kyle yelled from the living room. "You better hurry, or you'll miss your flight."

That didn't sound like such a bad idea, but she couldn't disappoint her parents by not showing up. They hadn't seen her since Easter. "I'll be right there," she told Kyle, and reluctantly picked up her suitcase.

He was standing by the front door as she put on her coat.

"Give me a call when you arrive so I'll know you got there all right."

His words helped warm the chill around her heart.

She longed to throw herself into his arms but, mindful of his crutches, she put her hands on his waist and kissed him. With a muffled groan he pulled her closer, deepening the kiss until it was a sharing of souls. His crutches fell to the floor with a loud clatter. Luckily, he was able to lean back against the wall in order to support himself and avoid falling, but it did bring their kiss to an end.

Cursing softly, he leaned against the low bookcase to his right while Victoria bent down and picked up the crutches from the floor. At one time he would have teased her by saying, "What are you trying to do, Tory, break my other ankle?" just as he had when he'd first arrived.

But this wasn't the time for teasing. It was the time for leaving.

She handed him the crutches one at a time and waited until he had them securely under his arms again. Although it probably wasn't the most opportune moment to be asking this question, she couldn't restrain herself. "Are you sure you'll be all right?"

"I'm fine," he growled.

She knew it was impatience that made his voice so rough, so she didn't take offense at his tone.

"Your cab is waiting," he reminded her.

She'd been drinking in the sight of him, storing it up for those moments when they'd be apart. "I'll be back late tomorrow night. Tell your brother I said hi." Rick was arriving later today but would only be staying one night. At least that meant that Kyle wouldn't be alone on Thanksgiving, although she would have loved to have him come up to Vermont with her. She'd asked him, including Rick in the invitation, but he'd pointed out that it had been a long time since he'd seen his brother, and he'd wanted to spend some time alone with him. After all, it was only one night and two days she was talking about here, not an eternity. Just thirty-five hours and forty-five minutes, that was all. But that didn't include the cab ride to and from the airport, the cab she was going to miss if she didn't get a move on.

"Go on," he prompted her. "I'll see you when you get back."

I love you. She didn't say the words aloud this time, but she said them silently as she gave him another quick kiss before grabbing her suitcase and hurrying out the door.

Victoria was surprised to find that she had a good time at her family's Thanksgiving Day bash. Her older brother

Tom claimed she was only smiling because she hadn't had to join in the preparations beforehand.

"Good planning on your part, Vicky," he said, knowing how she disliked the abbreviation of her name.

"I couldn't get an earlier flight, Tommy," she retorted, knowing how much *he* disliked being called *that*.

"Children, children." Mrs. Winters held up a wooden spoon as if it were a conductor's baton. "Victoria, why don't you finish setting out the silverware, and Tom, why don't you go help your father get some more chairs from the basement? It's just so good to have the whole family here again. I've missed the sound of you two arguing."

Victoria and Tom shared a grin. There had been a time when their mother hadn't been as sentimental about their teasing disputes. Absence must make the heart grow fonder. Victoria wondered if her absence would make Kyle's heart grow fonder. Was he missing her as much as she was missing him?

Just thinking about him brought a glow to her face that did not go unnoticed by other members of the family.

Never one to beat around the bush, Grandma Winters said, "You takin' some kind of special vitamins, child? Or are you in love?"

Everyone's eyes swiveled to a now-flushed Victoria. "Must be that vitamin C you told me to take," she replied, reluctant to discuss her private life in front of the entire clan.

But later, when her younger brother Andy cornered her, she didn't get away as easily.

"Does Kyle know about this guy you've fallen for?" Andy asked her.

"I think he does, yes."

"And does he approve?"

"Approve of the guy, you mean? Why, yes, I'm sure he thinks very highly of him." She smiled a secret smile. "He's often sung his praises to me, in fact."

"Good. I trust Kyle's judgment. You know, he'd make a great brother-in-law. Too bad you two don't see each other that way. What're you laughing at?"

She shook her head. "Nothing." She wasn't ready to come out and tell her family about the new relationship between herself and Kyle yet—it was still too fresh for her to share. But it was good to know that they'd approve. Or at least Andy would.

Her mother was the next one to bring up the subject of the possibility of a new man in Victoria's life. "Your grandmother is right, you do look happy. Are you seeing someone new?"

"I am seeing someone."

"Is it serious?"

"I hope so."

Seeing her mother's inquiring gaze, Victoria said, "I'm not ready to talk about it just yet. I don't want to jinx it or anything."

She was asked the same thing in various ways by at least another half-dozen relatives, her aunts, her cousins, even her six-year-old niece.

Never one to be left out, her older brother Tom asked bluntly, "So who is this guy?"

"Not another word if you value your life," she threatened him. "I've already been interrogated by half the Winterses from here to Burlington, including your daughter, who isn't even out of kindergarten yet! So unless you want me to tell Mom the truth about that bra she found in your car when you were sixteen, you'll drop the subject."

Her brother put his hand to his chest in a display of horror. "Not the bra threat! You wouldn't."

"I would."

He sighed. "Consider the subject dropped."

What actually began dropping that evening was heavy snow, and it didn't let up all the next day. The children were delighted, but Victoria was dismayed. She couldn't get snowbound up here, she just couldn't. The airport couldn't close, but it did. She called Kyle.

It wasn't the first time she'd spoken to him on the phone since she'd arrived in Vermont. She'd called him to say she'd gotten there safely, just as she'd promised she would. But he hadn't been able to talk to her very long because his brother had arrived in the middle of the conversation. She'd tried calling him several times since then, but there hadn't been any reply. She was relieved when he answered the phone after the first ring.

"Kyle!"

"Tory, what's wrong?"

"I'm sorry. I didn't mean to wail like that. It's just that we've got this awful snowstorm going on up here, and they've closed the airport. They've canceled my flight."

"Smart thing to do if the airport is closed," he replied.

"You don't understand. That means I won't be able to make it home tonight."

"That's okay."

"What do you mean, that's okay? The least you could do is say you miss me." She paused expectantly, but all she heard was strong static on the other end of the phone. "Kyle, can you hear me?"

"...tomorrow...anyway...for the best..." were the only words of his that she could hear.

Before she could say anything further, the phone line went dead.

"Hey, sis, I just heard on the radio that a lot of the phone lines are out," Andy said as he walked by with a turkey drumstick in one hand. "There's quite a wind kicking up out there. Looks like we're going to be here for a while."

It was Sunday afternoon before she was able to leave. She only got to the airport then because of the snowplow Tom had attached to the front of his four-wheel-drive pickup truck. The phones were still out at her parent's house, but they'd heard on the news that the airport was open and flights were departing. So Tom had volunteered to take her. Once they got on the major roads, the going was much easier than it had been in the mostly rural area where their parents lived.

To her surprise, Tom didn't just drop her off at curbside. Instead, he stayed and escorted her all the way to the gate. "I promised Mom I'd make sure you got off all right," he said with a self-conscious shrug.

She was glad for the company. Talking with Tom made the time until her flight was called go by faster.

"Take care of yourself." She hugged him fiercely. "And thanks for the ride."

"No problem. I just hope that this guy, whoever he is, realizes what he's got. And next time bring him with you."

Victoria was so eager to see Kyle again that even the short flight seemed never-ending. It had snowed in New York, as well, but only enough to make the roads slushy and snarl up traffic. The cab ride from the airport took almost as long as the flight had.

Bernie greeted her with a smile as he held open the cab door for her. "Welcome home, Miss Winters."

"It's good to be home, Bernie. For a while there I thought I'd never get out of Vermont."

"Thought you liked it up there."

"I do."

Bernie nodded sagaciously. "You missed Mr. O'Reilly. You two make a nice couple."

"Yes, we do, don't we?" she agreed with a grin. Now that she was home, her mood was greatly improved.

She was surprised to find that her hand was actually shaking with excitement as she pushed her key into the lock. "Kyle! I'm home!" she sung out the moment as she got inside. "Kyle?"

"I'm in here."

She followed the sound of his voice to the spare room, his room before he'd begun sharing her bedroom with her. He stood with his back to her, and the first thing she noticed was that he wasn't using his crutches. Instead, he was leaning on a cane. The cast on his ankle looked different, too. This must be the walking cast he'd told her about. She was about to comment on the change when Kyle moved slightly, and for the first time she got a look at what he was doing. "You're packing!"

"That's right."

"Why?"

"Global's put me back on active duty. I've got to catch a flight to Vancouver tonight."

It took several seconds for the news to sink in. Her confused mind scrambled for an explanation. "Did Angelica do this? Is she behind them shipping you out so soon?"

"No. I requested the assignment."

His words hit her with the force of a blow. "Wh-what?"

"I requested the assignment," he repeated, tossing another shirt into his suitcase.

"Why would you do something like that? Your ankle isn't even completely healed yet."

"Stop hovering." The words were almost the same as those he'd used numerous times before, but the inflection was entirely different. Where once there had been teasing affection, now there was flat impatience. His tone of voice clearly said, "Go away. Stop bothering me." It wounded her deeply.

"I don't understand." She blinked back the tears. "What happened? When I left on Thursday, everything was fine. Now I come home and find you packing. What's going on?"

"Nothing's going on. I've got a job to do, and I'm doing it." He closed the zip around his suitcase.

"When will you be back?"

"I'm not sure." He picked up his case and walked past her.

She followed him down the hallway toward the front door she'd just entered with such eagerness and was now looking at with such dread. "What about us?"

"We need some time apart, Tory. It's the best thing for both of us."

"Kyle, don't you dare walk out that door without giving me more of an explanation than that!"

She should have remembered that Kyle didn't respond well to dares. He kept right on going and didn't look back.

Eleven

"Victoria, get your head out of the freezer and talk to me," Sue demanded.

"I'm all out of chocolate chocolate-chip ice cream!" Victoria wailed, as if it meant the end of the world.

Sue recognized the signs. "How many cartons of ice cream have you gone through since Kyle left?"

"Four."

"And he only left yesterday." Sue shook her head. "Not good, Victoria. Here, eat some cookies instead and tell me what happened."

"I can't eat those cookies." Victoria sniffed as tears threatened to fall yet again. "Those are peanut butter cookies. Kyle's favorite."

"If you can't eat them, I will." Sue took a large bite out of one. "What on earth happened? I thought you two were making a go of things. When Kyle came to talk to me a few weeks ago and started asking me questions about you, I thought for sure he felt the same way you did."

"I thought so, too. But obviously he doesn't. I love him, Sue. And I made the mistake of telling him so. That's why he left. He felt I was pressuring him, telling him I loved him when he couldn't say the same about me."

"Did he say that?"

"Of course not."

"Then what did he say?"

"That we needed some time apart. That it's the best thing for both of us." Victoria repeated his words exactly. They were already permanently etched in her memory. She'd heard them over and over in her dreams last night, disturbing what little rest she'd gotten.

"That's all he said? No other explanation?"

"I told you. I came home from the airport and found him packing. If I'd have come home a few minutes later he would have left already. I probably would've come home to find a note waiting for me."

Sue frowned thoughtfully. "This doesn't sound like Kyle."

"You said yourself that we only knew Kyle as a friend, that he'd be very different in the role of lover."

"I didn't mean that he'd turn into a Dr. Jekyll and Mr. Hyde."

"He just doesn't love me. So he left. Maybe he was being cruel to be kind. He didn't want to string me along, so he walked out on me instead." Victoria paused before looking at Sue expectantly. "Well, aren't you going to argue with me? Tell me I'm wrong?"

"Sounds plausible to me."

"Thanks, you're a big help." Victoria opened the refrigerator door, searching for more chocolate.

"What do you want me to say? That men stink?"

"Do you think he would have left if I hadn't said I loved him?"

"You're driving yourself crazy with this, you know." Sue took a Sara Lee German chocolate cake away from her. "Did Kyle say when he'd be back?"

"He said he wasn't sure."

"Where did he go?"

"Vancouver."

"Well, at least he's still on the North American continent. Maybe he'll call you."

"Why should he?" Victoria countered. "You just said that he walked out on me."

"I didn't say that, you did."

"You agreed with me."

"Maybe he'll have second thoughts once he's away," Sue murmured. "Maybe he'll realize that he loves you, too."

"You really think so?" Sue's somewhat doubtful look made her reach for the cake again. "I'm never going to hear from him again, am I?" she said in bleak despair.

"Victoria, he still lives in this apartment, or at least he does when he's in the city. Of course you'll see him again. What about Christmas? He must get off for Christmas. Maybe he'll come home then."

"I don't want to hear any more maybes. Other women have fallen for men who don't love them in return. I'll get over it, in a million years or so. Maybe I should move out of this apartment. My being here is just going to make things awkward."

"Don't make any hasty decisions, okay? Wait and see how things are between you when Kyle comes back."

Another thought had just occurred to Victoria. "What if he comes back with another woman? What if he meets someone in Vancouver?"

"Let's try not to second-guess the future, it only gives you ulcers. You're under enough stress as it is. When was the last real meal you had?"

"I'm not hungry."

"Then why are you eating that cake as if there's no tomorrow?"

"Habit. I always eat chocolate when I'm depressed." The tears started again, and Victoria grabbed for the box of facial tissues she'd kept handy since Kyle's departure. "It hurts so damn much," she said unsteadily.

Sue hugged her with sisterly understanding. "I know it does. Go ahead and cry. Get it out of your system."

The problem was that Victoria didn't think she'd ever get Kyle out of her system. And the more time went by, the more convinced she was of that fact. She saw him everywhere. The apartment was filled with memories of him. She'd look at his collection of geodes and cry. She'd walk into the den and cry. She'd see a letter addressed to him and cry. She used up several bottles of eyedrops trying to clear up the bloodshot evidence of her crying jags. Despair, resentment, humiliation, pain, anger—it felt like a never-ending cycle.

Finally she was cried out. Then she felt numb. It was a state she welcomed. She kept on the go so much that she didn't have time to think about anything. The holidays were fast approaching, and the stores were gaily decorated to lure shoppers. She avoided them like the plague. She'd never felt less like celebrating, and she dreaded the merrymaking that went along with the Christmas season.

Her uncharacteristically Scrooge-like behavior did not go unnoticed by those around her.

"You all right, Miss Winters?" Bernie asked her as she came in late one Monday evening. "You seem very pale."

"I'm fine." Her flat answer alone would have told anyone who knew her that something was wrong. Under normal circumstances, Victoria always stopped and chatted with people.

"Have you heard when Mr. O'Reilly is coming home?"

"No."

Bernie tried again. "Will he be home for Christmas?"

"I have no idea."

"I'll bet you miss him."

Dead silence.

Bernie finally got the message that there was trouble in paradise.

Early the next Saturday morning, Victoria got a surprise visitor. It looked as though more trouble was on its way.

The call came from Bernie. "Miss Winters, there's a Mrs. Van Horne here to see you. Shall I send her up?"

Victoria didn't know what to say. Angelica was the last person she wanted to see.

"She says it's urgent," Bernie added.

Had something happened to Kyle? "All right, send her up."

Victoria was not her normal diplomatic self. "I was just on my way out," she coolly informed the other woman after opening the apartment door.

"You can relax," Angelica assured her. "I'm not here to start a fight. May I come in?"

Victoria reluctantly stood aside and let her enter. "Why *are* you here?"

"It's about Kyle."

"Is he all right?"

"I don't think so. I think he's trying to work himself into an early grave." Seeing how Victoria's face paled, she relented. "Well, maybe I am exaggerating a little, but it was foolish of him to go back to work so soon."

"I'm sure Kyle knows what he's doing."

"I'm sure he does. But do *you* know what he's doing? Working twelve-hour days. And do you know why? Because he loves you."

Victoria had to sit down to keep from falling down. "You came here to tell me Kyle loves me?"

Angelica nodded. "I know it sounds strange, after what's gone on recently. But you and Kyle made me realize what I was doing wrong."

"We did?"

Angelica nodded.

"Forgive me for being a little doubtful here, but I wouldn't have thought that either Kyle or myself were exactly your favorite people."

"You mean that little incident with your boss. I apologize for that. I shouldn't have done it. But I was jealous."

"Of me?"

"No, of what you and Kyle had together. It's what my husband and I used to have, what I wanted us to have again. It was a classic case, really, or so my therapist tells me. I was trying to make my husband jealous by seeing other men, by getting from them the love and the attention I needed and wasn't getting from my husband. It didn't work, of course, but I didn't realize how destructive my behavior had become until Kyle made me face myself and my actions. Since then I've gone into therapy and I've gotten my husband to join me. It's not an instant cure, but we're going to make it, I know we are. Anyway, I didn't come here to talk about my marriage, I came here to talk about you and Kyle. I don't know what went wrong between you, but I do know that I've never seen two people who loved each other more. What you've got is worth fighting for. Just promise me you'll think about what I've said."

"I will."

Victoria thought about it, but she couldn't agree with Angelica's analysis of the situation. So Kyle was working twelve-hour days in Vancouver—that didn't mean he loved her. There were any number of reasons he could be working so hard. Maybe he was trying to forget what had happened between them, maybe he felt guilty at having to hurt her, maybe he just had a lot of work to do!

The love that Angelica claimed she'd seen between them had been real on Victoria's part, but not on Kyle's. If he'd loved her, he wouldn't have left her. He wouldn't have voluntarily requested an assignment on the other side of the continent. And if he'd loved her, he wouldn't have reacted the way he had when she'd told him she loved him. No, Angelica's view of the situation must have been prejudiced by her own renewed happiness. Victoria knew from bitter experience that when you were in love and things were going your way the whole world seemed filled with love. She knew, too, that it was only an illusion.

A few days later she got a call from Sue. "The gang has decided that we all need something to cheer us up, so we're having an impromptu Christmas party. We've rented a suite at that new hotel that's just opened. You've got to come. It's tomorrow night. Do you know that

Jeff's talking about taking a job in London and George thinks he's going to be transferred to D.C. next month? This may be the last time we can all get together."

"Will Kyle be there?" Victoria's tone of voice made it clear that if Kyle was coming, she wasn't.

"George reached him up in Vancouver, but Kyle said he can't get the time off."

"So he's definitely not coming back for the holidays?" Victoria had been half holding her breath for fear that Kyle might show up unexpectedly at the apartment.

"That's what George said. So you'll come?"

Victoria twisted the phone cord around her finger. "I don't know."

"You don't have a choice. You can either come peaceably or I'll come over there and drag you out. Come on, it'll be fun. There'll be a lot of people there. Who knows, you may meet someone new. We'll even order in lots of chocolate chocolate-chip ice cream," Sue promised.

"I've sworn off it."

"Chocolate-chip cookies?"

"Those, too."

"What about my curry dip? Or honey-roasted cashews?"

Victoria sighed. Sue obviously wasn't going to give up. "Okay, you convinced me. What time?"

"Seven."

"Should I bring anything?"

"Just yourself. See you there."

But by the time the next evening rolled around, Victoria had already decided that she wouldn't be able to face a roomful of people—even if some of them were her close friends. Besides, it wasn't fair to ruin everyone else's holiday with her rotten mood. She called Sue at the hotel.

"Sue..."

"Victoria, where are you? You're late!"

"I'm calling from the airport, Sue. Listen, I'm sorry, but I'm just not in the mood to celebrate. I know you'll understand. I've taken a few extra days off work so that I can fly home early for Christmas. I just need to get away for a while. My flight's boarding, I've got to go. Your Christmas present's in the mail. So are George and Jeff's. I'll call you when I get back. Bye."

Sue hung up and turned to face a determined-looking Kyle. "She's not coming. She's flying home to Vermont instead. Now what?"

"I go after her."

Unfortunately, there wasn't a flight out until the next morning, so Kyle was forced to cool his heels overnight in the apartment. The place seemed so empty without Victoria. Everywhere he looked he was reminded of her. The grapefruit juice in the refrigerator, her silky underwear hanging over the shower rod, the smell of her perfume.

It was a night meant for playing the blues, but he hadn't been able to play the harmonica since he'd left. He hadn't even taken it out of its case. It, like so many other things, reminded him too much of Tory.

He hadn't stayed at the Christmas party once he'd found out she wasn't coming. His friends had understood his need to be alone. He appreciated the help they'd given him in setting things up. He was just sorry that it hadn't worked out the way he'd planned. But then, nothing had lately.

When Kyle landed at the airport in Burlington, Vermont, he hit another snag. It was only then that he realized he wasn't sure how to get out to Tory's parents' place. Oh, he knew the name of the small town, and he had a general idea of how to get there, but he didn't know the exact address. He tried calling, but their phone number was unlisted. Tory had given him her parents' number when she'd come up for Thanksgiving, but he hadn't thought to bring it along with him.

He shrugged and headed for the car-rental information desk. He was sure he'd remember where the house was once he was back in the area. After all, he'd been up here once before with Tory a few years ago. Of course, it had been summer then, but how much difference could that make?

A lot, he soon found out. Nothing looked familiar to him now that it was covered with several inches of snow. At least the weather and the roads were clear, not that that helped him much. After driving around in circles for an hour, he had another brainstorm. He suddenly remembered that Tory's older brother Tom ran the family hardware store in town. All he had to do was find Tom, and he would lead him to Tory. This time he had no trouble finding what he was looking for. The hardware store was the only one in town, and the name Winters on the sign was a dead giveaway.

"You say you're here to surprise Victoria?" Tom asked him after greeting him warmly. The two men had met during Kyle's previous visit.

"That's right."

"Well, she could use some cheering up, that's for sure. She's been downright morose since she got in last night. Mom's real worried about her. Do you know anything about this guy she's fallen for? Is that the reason she's so depressed?"

Kyle's heart plummeted. What guy was Tom talking about? He'd only been in Vancouver three weeks. She couldn't have met someone that quickly, could she? And without telling Sue or George or Jeff? She wouldn't keep something like that to herself, would she?

"What makes you think she's fallen for some guy?" Kyle cautiously asked Tom.

"Because she was practically glowing while she was here for Thanksgiving, and now she's acting like her best friend's died. You're a good friend of hers. You mean you don't know what's going on, either?"

"I've been away a lot lately."

"Maybe she'll talk to you."

Kyle gave a fervent prayer and said, "I certainly hope so."

Victoria was up to her elbows in soapy dishwater when she heard her mother say, "There's someone here to see you, Victoria."

"Who is it?" she asked without turning around.

"It's me, Tory."

The dish she'd been washing slipped out of her hand and landed with a loud clatter in the sink. Luckily, it was made of a space-age material that didn't break. Victoria wished she were half as durable.

She turned slowly, almost afraid to believe her ears. No, she wasn't hearing things. Kyle was indeed standing in her parents' kitchen—without benefit of crutches, a cane or any sign of a cast. She blinked. He was still there when she opened her eyes. She wasn't hallucinating.

"Kyle decided to surprise you," her mother said.

"He succeeded," she croaked.

Her mother beamed. "I told you she'd be glad to see you," she told Kyle. "I've invited him to stay in Tom's old room," she told Victoria. "Please, sit down, Kyle."

She held out a kitchen chair for him. "Can I get you anything? Some coffee, some tea maybe?"

"I have everything I need," he replied, his eyes on Victoria.

Mrs. Winters nodded. "I'll leave you two alone then. I'm sure you must have lots to catch up on."

The kitchen was deathly quiet after she left. Kyle noticed with a pang that Victoria avoided looking at him. For the first time he wondered if he'd done the right thing in coming.

"Why are you here?" she finally asked him in a nervous voice.

"I had to see you."

"You could have seen me in New York. Why come all the way up here?"

"You left before I could see you in New York."

"I thought you were spending the holidays in Vancouver. Sue said you were too busy to come home." Victoria stopped speaking as something clicked in her mind. "Wait a minute. That party last night was a setup, wasn't it? Sue knew you'd be there!"

He nodded.

"I don't understand. Why the elaborate charade?"

"I told you, I wanted to see you."

"All you had to do was come to the apartment. I'm not exactly hard to find," she noted sarcastically.

"I wanted us to meet on neutral ground."

"Why? So you can tell me you want me to move out of the apartment? It's all right, I've already started looking around for another place."

"No, I don't want you to move!"

"I really think I should. Under the circumstances it would be the best thing for both of us."

He winced when he heard his own words tossed back at him. "Tory, we need to talk."

"If you'd wanted to talk you could have picked up a phone and called me. They do have phones in Vancouver, don't they?"

"What I have to say has to be said face-to-face."

Victoria paled. She didn't like the sound of that one bit. It sounded final.

"Is there some place where we can talk without being interrupted?" he asked her.

She wanted to say no. She didn't want to have this conversation with him. She didn't want it to end this way. But she could see that he was determined. "We can talk in the other room. We won't be disturbed there."

She led him to a small sitting room facing the backyard.

"Well?" She turned to face him.

"Give me a minute. This isn't as easy as I thought it would be."

"Breaking up is rarely easy," she retorted bitterly.

"Who's breaking up?"

"We are."

"Says who?"

"Says you."

"No, I don't." He shook his head in confusion. "Is that why you're so distant? Because you think I'm here to break it off? Tory, why would I fly thousands of miles from Vancouver to break up with you? I could have done that over the phone. Hell, I could have done that by not coming after you at all."

"Then why are you here?"

"Because you once told me you loved me, and I need to know if you were telling the truth. And I don't mean loving me as a friend, I mean loving me as a man."

But Victoria had no intention of leaving herself open for pain again. "Why don't you go first for a change? Tell me how *you* feel about *me*."

"All right, I will. I love you, not only as a friend but as a woman, the woman I want to spend the rest of my life with. *Now* will you tell me how you feel?"

"I already told you I loved you! I thought that's why you left. Because I'd pressured you."

"I left because you took the words back as soon as you said them. And you weren't exactly thinking clearly the first time you did say them. I thought you'd declared something in a moment of passion that you'd clearly regretted and hadn't meant."

"I only took the words back because of the expression on your face. You looked like I'd just kicked you."

"It's called shock, Tory. I wasn't expecting you to say the words so soon, and I never meant for you to say them first. I had it all planned, a romantic candlelight dinner for two, champagne, the whole thing. And then you blew me away by saying you loved me and then saying you didn't really mean it and then explaining at length how you only loved me like a friend. I could've throttled you!"

She thought of all the anguish, the pain, and she could have throttled him—if she hadn't loved him so much. "Why didn't you tell me this then? Why did you walk out on me?"

"I didn't walk out, I said we needed some time apart. I was hoping you'd miss me and realize you did love me after all. When I didn't hear from you I wanted to come back, but Sue told me how angry you were. So I thought it would be better to surprise you by showing up at the party—but then you blew that plan by flying up here instead."

"I wasn't in the mood to celebrate then," she admitted.

"And now?"

"Now I think I'll go crazy if you don't kiss me soon."

She'd no sooner spoken the words than he'd pulled her into his arms. Their lips met with a hunger made more intense by the time they'd been apart. Somehow, neither one was exactly sure how, they ended up sitting on the small couch. The kiss continued, uninterrupted by the move.

Victoria felt as if she'd come home. This was where she belonged—in his arms. She wanted to stay there forever. She moved even closer, impatient of the material that separated them.

Kyle suddenly felt someone tapping him on the shoulder. He knew it wasn't Victoria, because both her hands were beneath his shirt. Victoria also felt someone tapping her on the shoulder, and she knew it wasn't Kyle, because both his hands were on the buttons of her blouse. Startled, they both turned to see a pair of pixieish eyes staring at them over the back of the couch.

"Whatcha doin'?" Victoria's six-year-old niece Maria asked with bright-eyed interest.

Luckily the sound of Mrs. Winters's voice saved them from having to answer. "Maria, where are you? I've got some cookies for you."

In a flash the little girl raced out of the room.

Kyle gave Victoria a meaningful look. "Can we go some place a little more private?"

She nodded. "I know just the place. Come on." Taking him by the hand, she led him to the front door where they quickly put on their down coats. "Mother, Kyle and I are going Christmas shopping," she called out. "We'll be back late!"

* * *

"Some kind of Christmas shopping," Kyle murmured, nuzzling her bare shoulder.

"You didn't like your present?" she questioned provocatively.

"Mmm." His husky growl and blissful smile confirmed his satisfaction.

They were in a beautifully furnished room in a small country inn about an hour's drive from her parents' house. The bed was huge, with a romantic canopy of white lace. The innkeeper had given them the honeymoon suite. It was the only room he'd had available.

They'd just made love. And it had been better than ever before, because each caress had been backed by the certainty that they loved each other. They'd both spoken the words aloud frequently, chasing away the pain of their separation. He'd taken her to the very edge of ecstasy before making her his, just as she'd made him hers. She'd enfolded him deep within her, welcoming him, enveloping him, loving him. Together they'd experienced the ultimate pinnacle of physical joy—the heavy anticipation, the taut release, the spiraling free fall. Now they lay in each other's arms, marvelously satisfied, quietly enjoying the pleasure of just holding each other.

"I've got something for you," Kyle whispered in her ear.

She traced a languid hand down his hip. "So soon? We just—"

He gave a sexy laugh. "I'm not talking about that, I'm talking about this." He leaned over her and reached for his slacks, which lay in a heap on the floor. He dug into the pocket and came away with a box in his hand. A jeweler's box.

"You remember how you kept asking me what I told your boss when I called him?"

She nodded, her eyes glued to the box he held in his hand.

"I think it's time that I told you."

Victoria looked at him in confusion. Her boss was the last subject she wanted to talk about.

"I told him that I wanted to marry you. I told him that you hadn't agreed yet, but that I was sure you soon would—providing I didn't push you too hard. Then I swore him to secrecy, and, being the good diplomat that he is, he kept his word."

"Why did you tell him that?"

"Because it was the truth. I do want you to marry me. You haven't agreed yet—"

"You haven't asked me yet," she pointed out.

"You mean I've got to actually *ask* you? On bended knee and all that?"

She nodded. "I kind of like the idea."

He gave a long-suffering sigh and reluctantly shoved the covers aside.

She missed him before he'd even moved four inches. "On second thought, you can stay where you are, but you still have to ask me."

"Victoria Alison Winters, will you do me the great honor of being my wife?"

Now that the moment had arrived, her throat suddenly dried up. Hearing him actually say the words had a powerful effect on her. She couldn't speak.

"What?" he asked when she mumbled something incoherent.

She nodded.

"Yes?" he asked.

The word finally came out. "Yes!"

"Great. Then, since you answered that question correctly, you get to keep this." He opened the box and showed her the ring. It was a beautiful diamond in a wonderfully old-fashioned setting. "Do you like it?"

"I love it! I've never seen anything like it."

"That's because it's a copy of the original design my grandfather gave my grandmother. You seemed to think their story was romantic when I told you about their meeting at Ellis.... But maybe you'd rather have a more modern ring."

"Oh, Kyle!" She threw her arms around him. "This is the best ring you could have given me. It's perfect. Or it will be when you put it on my finger." She held out her hand.

His fingers were shaking almost as badly as hers, but he slipped the ring on without any trouble. "It fits."

"Perfectly." Her smile was radiant."

"I wasn't sure you'd say yes, you know. In fact, when I first came up here I thought I didn't have a chance."

"And now?"

"And now..." He lifted her hand to his lips and kissed her fingers. "I think you'll be wearing that ring at least as long as my grandmother's been wearing hers."

"Fifty years."

"Fifty-*five* years," he corrected her, lowering her back down onto the bed.

"I'm looking forward to every one of them!"

* * * * *

ATTRACTIVE, SPACE SAVING BOOK RACK

Display your most prized novels on this handsome and sturdy book rack. The hand-rubbed walnut finish will blend into your library decor with quiet elegance, providing a practical organizer for your favorite hard-or soft-covered books.

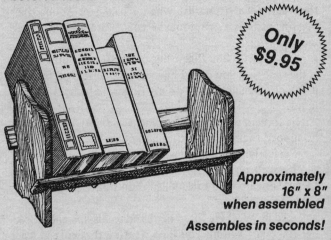

Only $9.95

Approximately 16" x 8" when assembled

Assembles in seconds!

To order, rush your name, address and zip code, along with a check or money order for $10.70* ($9.95 plus 75¢ postage and handling) payable to *Silhouette Books*.

Silhouette Books
Book Rack Offer
901 Fuhrmann Blvd.
P.O. Box 1396
Buffalo, NY 14269-1396

Offer not available in Canada.

*New York and Iowa residents add appropriate sales tax.

Silhouette Desire

COMING NEXT MONTH

#445 PASSION'S CHILD—Ann Major
Book One of the CHILDREN OF DESTINY trilogy!
Amy Holland and Nick Browning's marriage of convenience could turn to passion—if the secret of their child was not revealed....

#446 ISLAND HEAT—Suzanne Forster
When Justin Dunne's search led him to a "haunted castle" and beautiful Lauren Cambridge, he knew it wasn't the right time to get involved, unless he could mix business *and* pleasure.

#447 RAZZMATAZZ—Patricia Burroughs
Being stranded in the Reno airport left Kennie Sue Ledbetter with limited options. Alexander Carruthers came to her rescue, and somehow the next morning she found herself married...to him!

#448 TRUE COLORS— Mary Blayney
It would take all of television heartthrob Tom Wineski's considerable charm to convince small-town single mother Janelle Harper he'd developed a forever kind of passion.

#449 A TASTE OF HONEY—Jane Gentry
Susannah Reid was content with her life...until notorious Jefferson Cody hit town. He convinced her to start thinking about her own happiness—not what the neighbors would say.

#450 ROUGHNECK—Doreen Owens Malek
Beau Landry was a direct contrast to refined lawyer Morgan Taylor. Beau had done the wrong thing for the right reason, but when he proposed, would Morgan approve of his tactics?

AVAILABLE NOW:

#439 THE CASTLE KEEP
Jennifer Greene

#440 OUT OF THE COLD
Robin Elliott

#441 RELUCTANT PARTNERS
Judith McWilliams

#442 HEAVEN SENT
Erica Spindler

#443 A FRIEND IN NEED
Cathie Linz

#444 REACH FOR THE MOON
Joyce Thies

Don't miss the enchanting
TALES OF THE RISING MOON
A Desire trilogy by Joyce Thies

MOON OF THE RAVEN—June (#432)
Conlan Fox was part American Indian and as tough as the Montana land he rode, but it took fragile yet strong-willed Kerry Armstrong to make his dreams come true.

REACH FOR THE MOON—August (#444)
It would take a heart of stone for Steven Armstrong to evict the woman and children living on his land. But when Steven saw Samantha, eviction was the last thing on his mind!

GYPSY MOON—October (#456)
Robert Armstrong met Serena when he returned to his ancestral estate in Connecticut. Their fiery temperaments clashed from the start, but despite himself, Rob was falling under the Gypsy's spell.

To order Joyce Thies's MOON OF THE RAVEN (#432), or REACH FOR THE MOON (#444) send your name, address and zip or postal code, along with a check or money order for $2.50 for each book ordered, plus 75¢ postage and handling, payable to Silhouette Reader Service to:

In Canada	In U.S.A
P.O. Box 609	901 Fuhrmann Blvd.
Fort Erie, Ontario	P.O. Box 1396
L2A 5X3	Buffalo, NY 14269-1396

Please specify book title with your order.